Jack's Head

SIGGY SHADE

Trigger Warnings

Attempted sexual coercion
    Breeding play
    Decapitation
    Degradation
    Humiliation
    Murder
    Mutilation
    Object insertion (deadly weapons)
    Insertion with unusual appendages]
    Percussion play
    Pony play
    Public nudity
    Public sex
    Trafficking (brief mention)

Chapter One

The silk blindfold is tied so tight I can't see a peep of light. I stretch my hands out and feel my way through the party. William's Halloween bash is in full swing, yet he's chosen now to lead me to a surprise.

Chatter fills my ears, mingled with the strains of *The Monster Mash*. I brush shoulders with the other guests.

"Where are we going?" I yell over the music.

William kneads my shoulders with his large hands. "Bedroom."

"What's the surprise?"

"Naughty naughty, Bess." He pats my ass. "You'll find out when we get there."

My pulse quickens, and an excited shiver runs down my spine to settle between my legs. William proposed last night with a five-carat diamond solitaire. I accepted, of course.

"Is it lingerie?"

"Something to put in your mouth," he whispers in my ear.

I grin. "A chocolate eclair?"

He snickers. "Saltier but a similar shape."

1

I lick my lips at the prospect of William's cock. He probably wants to play out the erotic story we read about the highwayman and the tavern wench.

"We had the whole day together in the office," I ask. "Why now?"

I'm not just William's fiancée but his executive assistant. That means organizing everything from his travel arrangements to lavish parties like this one at his ancestral home. My outstretched fingers brush against wood, and William opens the door, filling my nostrils with the combined scents of cinnamon, cloves, nutmeg, and ginger.

I step over the threshold. Before I can ask why he lit the pumpkin spice candles, he moves away, removing his warmth from my back.

"Surprise," he whispers.

I pull off the blindfold and glance around his mahogany-paneled bedroom. He leans against the wall clad in his black tricorn hat, mask, and cloak. He's dressed like Sixteen String Jack, the headless highwayman rumored to haunt the neighborhood every Halloween in search of a new head.

"What's the surprise, then?" I place my hands on my hips, taking in his long leather boots and golden buckles.

"You make a wonderful tavern wench." His gaze drops to my cleavage spilling out of my low-cut white top.

Heat rises to my cheeks. Getting the costume was easy, but it took ages to arrange my unruly red curls into a half-braid crown. With a wiggle of my shoulders, I smooth my hands down the leather corset and voluminous skirt.

"Like it?"

"And I'm not the only one," he replies with a smirk.

"What do you mean?"

He turns me around, just as the bathroom door opens, revealing two stocky men. And they're wearing the same highwayman's costume as my fiancé. It takes several blinks to recognize his uncles, Thomas and Samuel.

My brow furrows. Those two are a pain in the ass. They never let us forget they hold fifty percent of the firm's voting rights until William turns thirty. Neither of them knows anything about finance, yet they won't stop meddling in the business.

"What's going on?" I ask.

William kneads my tense shoulder muscles. "Now that you're joining the family, it's time to show off your legendary fellatio skills."

Samuel beckons with a gloved hand. "Make it good, and we'll approve William's choice of fiancée."

Thomas unclasps his cloak. Beneath, he's naked, save for a pair of black leather boots. He's a six-foot-four former rugby player who's as broad as he is tall and loves to intimidate with his bulk.

And he's stroking a stubby cock that, even when erect, barely extends past his fist.

My stomach plummets, and I slap a hand over my mouth. My fiancé wants to pimp me out to his uncles?

"William." It comes out as a croak.

He gives me a gentle push. "Everyone expects me to be with a ten who's tall and blonde and lovely. Do you know why I chose you above all others?" He doesn't give me the chance to answer. "Your open mind. No man wants to be with a prude."

"But..."

My words falter because there's so much to unpack, yet nothing he's said makes sense. I turn to meet his pale-blue eyes blazing with heat, and the expectation that I won't disappoint him in front of his uncles.

"W-what made you think I would agree to this?" The

words catch in my throat because I can't believe he wants to share me with his fucking relatives.

"Bess." He waves his hand toward the older men. "This is just like the novella we read together last month. You said it was hot."

My jaw drops. "But that was fiction!"

I knew this relationship was too good to be true. Secretaries only end up with the executive in movies, but William had assured me those long hours we'd spent together had created a bond that surpassed differences like social class.

His parents died in a car crash last year, leaving me to guide him through the running of the family firm. We had the same taste in music, movies, and manga. We worked so closely and so well that I thought we had a connection.

My chest burns with betrayal, the sensation filling my throat with bile. It presses down on my lungs and flattens my heart. I swallow back a bitter mouthful and try to keep breathing.

Even when our relationship got sexual, part of me waited for a catch. But William claimed to love my fuller figure and my attitude toward sex. We used to read smutty books together and try out the spicy scenes.

This is a fucking ambush. I step back, my limbs trembling, my gaze darting to the middle-aged men stroking their cocks. "This isn't happening."

"Bess," William flashes his teeth. "If you want to remain my fiancée, you need to bring more to the table than a bad attitude."

My nostrils flare. "What's that supposed to mean?"

"You're a great assistant and an even better fuck. But looks-wise, you're a five at best."

The words hit like a punch to the gut, and every muscle in my body stiffens. This isn't the first time William has disparaged my looks, but he also adds that I make up for it by being the best he's ever had in bed. Fuck. All the pieces are finally coming together. He only ever wanted me for sex. Sex with his uncles.

I turn on my heel and stride toward the door.

"If you leave, it's over," he says to my retreating back. "Not just our engagement, but your employment at Whitechapel Finance."

My throat tightens, and I turn to meet his smirk.

The two older men chuckle. William tips his head, his eyes twinkling. They think I'm cornered.

"Go fuck yourself," I snap. "Better still, fuck them."

"Why are you getting cold feet all of a sudden?" William grabs my arm. "You're usually game for anything."

The laugh I huff is bitter. William apparently has hidden a side that enjoys degradation and coercion. Tears sting the backs of my eyes. If I were quick-witted, I'd strike back with something cutting. But I'm more of a doer than a thinker and better with my hands than I am with words.

I yank my arm out of his grip. "I'd rather suck a corpse than go anywhere near your relatives' rancid cocks."

His smug expression drops. "Bess?"

"If you think I'm sticking around to be demeaned, you've got another thing coming." I fling the door open, letting in the strains of *Thriller*.

The hallway is filled with partygoers in fancy dress sipping cocktails and nibbling canapés.

At the sight of them, relief loosens my tight muscles and quickens my steps. William won't make a scene. Everyone at this party is connected to Whitechapel Finance. He wouldn't dare let the public know he's a predator. I push my way through the throng, ignoring the murmured congratulations on my engagement.

My throat tightens as I descend the grand staircase, with

5

William on my heels, each step a silent goodbye to Whitechapel Manor.

"Do you realize what you stand to lose?" he hisses as we cross the black-and-white-tiled entrance hall.

Everything. My fiancé, my financial security, my future. I should never have let that bastard persuade me to give up my lease—now, I'm not just homeless, I'm screwed.

He follows me through the double doors and out into the night.

A cool breeze blows through the trees and hedgerows surrounding Whitechapel Manor. I inhale, filling my lungs with fresh air. The moon is full with a thin veil of clouds, but with more than enough light to drive through the unlit country roads to find a hotel.

William grabs the back of my braid. "That's it?" he asks with a hiss. "You'll throw away our relationship, your reputation, and everything you've worked for, over a tantrum?"

Dread wraps around my neck like a noose. How the bloody hell is he planning to ruin my reputation?

I dig my fingernails into the back of his hand, making him release my hair with a curse. It's strange how a man can be non-violent until the moment he doesn't get complete obedience. I continue walking and slip into my Volkswagen Beetle.

William pulls the door open, as though that will stop me from leaving. It won't.

"Halloween is too dangerous for you to drive alone," he says, sounding smug. "Headless Jack haunts the roads, hunting for people to kill. At least stay until morning."

"So you can coerce me into getting on my knees?" I yank the door closed, start the engine, and pull out of the parking spot.

"You're fired," William yells loud enough to reach me through the closed window. "And you're no longer entitled to a company car. Come back inside, or I'll have you arrested for motor theft."

Shit.

I pull out down the driveway. William will run the company into the ground in six months without my help. It's not like he can turn to his uncles for advice—they're always looking for excuses to make him feel incompetent.

"You'll never work again with a criminal record!" he bellows.

I drive through the manor's iron gates, blood roaring in my ears. I glance into the rearview mirror to find William standing in the courtyard, already on the phone.

How much do I want to bet my soon-to-be-bleak future that he's calling the police?

I snatch my gaze away and take a left onto a country road. With all that money and influence at his disposal, William could make my life a living nightmare. I try to console myself with the thought that I've left a relationship before it became abusive, but all I feel is mounting dread.

Misery thickens my throat and self-pity clouds my vision with tears. I clench my teeth and shove those emotions into the pit of my stomach. I refuse to cry over that asshole.

Moments later, the temperature drops, and a flash of silver lights up my periphery. I glance at the rearview mirror to find the road empty, save for a glowing horseman.

And he's galloping toward me, a foot above the tarmac.

Chapter Two

T he ground beneath my Beetle's tires changes from smooth to bumpy, bringing my attention back to the road. I should have reached the highway by now, but I'm still driving down a single-track lane bordered by tall trees. My gaze flicks to the rearview mirror, where the horseman rides toward me.

"That can't be right," I whisper.

Laser light shows don't move down roads unless there's a traveling projector, and it's just me and what's beginning to look like a ghost.

That's when I remember William's warning: It's Halloween. The night when headless Jack haunts the roads, hunting for someone to kill. A high-pitched neigh fills my ears, making my heart jump into my throat. My fingers fumble over the stereo, only to find it already turned off.

"What the fuck?" Stomping my foot on the gas, I put as much distance between me and whatever's out there. Ghosts usually haunt specific places, like houses or small stretches of road, so it should be only a matter of time before I leave his domain. Everything will be all right as soon as I reach the highway.

I'm doing fifty miles an hour on a country lane. The trees and hedgerows on either side have been replaced by gnarled oaks with twisting branches.

I accelerate to sixty, then seventy, but as the speedometer reaches eighty, a dark mass jumps over the car. It lands several feet ahead with the thud of hoofbeats hitting dirt. I slam my foot on the brake and scream.

In the middle of the road ahead dances a black horse with eyes of fire and a mane of smoke. It stands over eight feet tall and looks like it could trample my Beetle to dust.

More worrying is its rider. He wears a similar highway-man's costume to William's but the cloak is frayed. In one hand, he carries a double-headed ax, and in the other a jack o'lantern filled with flames.

Cold shivers run down my spine. There's a void above his shoulders. He doesn't have a head!

I shift into reverse, twist toward the rear window, and speed back down the road. The horseman places the jack o'lantern on his shoulders and rides forward.

"Fuck."

He's no longer a silver specter—he's real. And he's advancing toward me with that ax.

I grope around the front seat for my phone, only to remember that I left it at William's. Right now, I'd rather face down a whole bedroom of naked uncles than this.

"Faster," I rev the engine. I don't bother to check my speed because that would mean looking at the phantom behind the windscreen. I press down on the accelerator. "Come on, move!"

The car hits an invisible barrier with a hard jolt. I whip my head around to see the horseman jumping off his steed.

Terror kicks me in the gut and every drop of blood in

my face drains toward my galloping heart. Should I run back to Whitechapel Manor? Should I scream in the hope that it scares him and his horse away?

Who the fuck am I trying to kid?

I can't outrun a man, let alone a horseman that can do eighty. And he probably gets off on a woman's shrieks.

Clomp, clomp, clomp.

His heavy footsteps shake the car. He's the tallest man I've ever seen and worryingly solid.

If I don't make a move this instant, William's revenge will be the least of my problems. With fingers that won't stop trembling, I ease the gear stick back into drive and stamp on the accelerator.

The car lurches, speeding toward the horseman. I'm going to ram him down.

William's probably already reported me for car theft. Can I afford to make things worse with a hit and run?

I tell that thought to go fuck itself. Anyone riding a demonic horse capable of turning from silver to solid has to be supernatural. Vehicular homicide doesn't apply to the dead.

"Stand and deliver!" shouts a voice deep enough to penetrate my bones. "Your noggin or your life."

How the hell does he expect to take someone's head without taking their life?

I grit my teeth and snarl, "No. Fucking. Way."

The horseman holds his ax like he's about to take a swing. A swing at my head.

I pull right to swerve out of the trajectory of his ax, but the steering wheel won't budge. My pulse quickens. In a few seconds, I'll become headless—just like him. Instead, I duck, just as his blade slices through glass and metal, cutting through the roof like a tin of corned beef.

Cold air blasts over my scalp. An even colder hand grabs

me by the neck and lifts me out of my seat. I squeeze my eyes shut and gasp.

"I have you now," he booms.

A scream tears out from deep within my soul. It's guttural, raw, primal. I thrash my arms and legs, trying to break free of his grip, but his fingers tighten around my throat.

"Look upon the face of your demise," he roars.

I shake my head. It's bad enough that I'm in the grip of an evil spirit who wants me dead. The bodice of my blouse flops open, exposing even more cleavage to the cold. I sure as fuck don't want my last memory on earth to be the swing of some accursed ax.

With a shuddering breath, I wait for the blade to strike, but he hesitates. From the way his flames warm my breasts, it's not a stretch to imagine why.

The horseman pulls me into his chest, filling my nostrils with the scent of sulfur–probably because he's fresh out of hell. I've got to act fast. My life flashes before my eyes. Vague recollections of the parents who died when I was four, followed by a bleak childhood spent in foster homes.

A cool breeze whips around my body, making my nipples tighten. I shove those memories aside. If I don't think fast, I'm going to wind up worse than dead.

Why isn't William here, being threatened instead of me? He'd probably offer me up to the headless horseman for a blowjob.

Wait—that's not a bad idea.

I slip my hand through the folds of his cloak, and over a silk shirt that covers a muscular torso.

He doesn't react until my fingers skim his breeches. The grip on my neck loosens, allowing me to breathe.

My pulse beats a rapid drumroll. It's now or never. I

slide my hand down his crotch, my fingers tracing the outline of a cock almost as thick as my wrist.

Bloody hell.

At his sharp intake of breath, I crack open an eye to lock gazes with a pumpkin as long as my head and twice as broad. Yellow flames flicker from its triangular eyes and from a broad mouth carved with jagged teeth.

My gaze wanders to the top, where a thick stalk curls backward, surrounded by withered leaves that simulate hair.

Fuck.

Self-preservation kicks me in the ass. I should be seducing, not scrutinizing. As I give his cock a gentle squeeze, a groan reverberates through his broad chest. The flames that fill the pumpkin's eyes and mouth burn brighter, bathing my face with warmth.

"Do you like that?" I ask, my voice husky.

The shiver down his huge body says he does. He places me carefully on my feet, the way a gentleman might help a lady out of a carriage.

My survival instincts scream at me to keep going. "There's more where that came from." I lick my lips and hope to god I sound lusty. "Now, let me see your other head."

His chest reverberates with a deep rumble that borders on a growl. My skin tingles with trepidation, and every hair on my body stands alert.

"Show me what else you can do, wench," he growls, the sound going to the pulse between my legs. "Impress me, and I will spare your life."

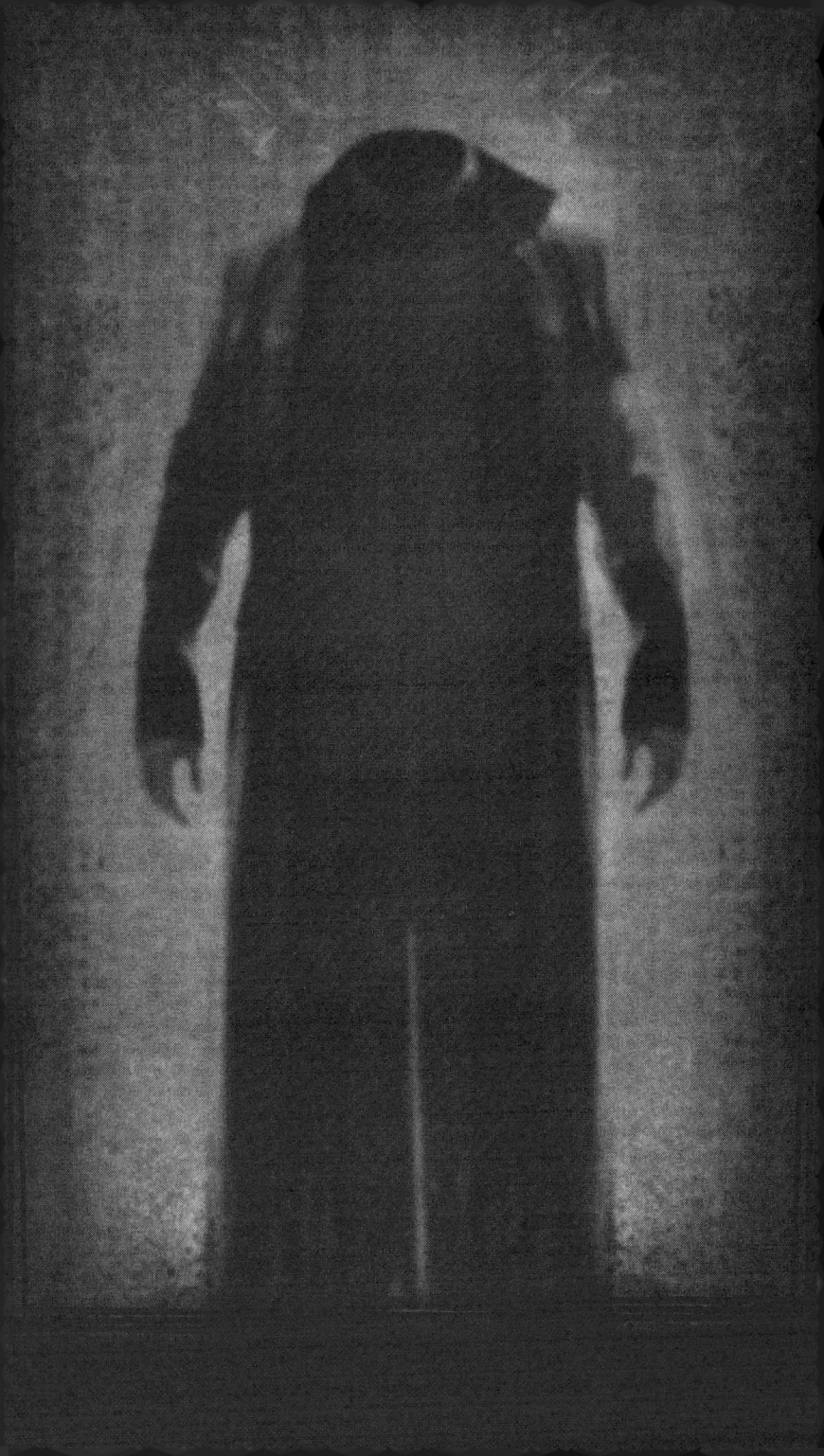

Chapter Three

⁓⌇⌇⁓

T he headless horseman pulls me into his broad chest like he's the hero of a bodice ripper, and I'm his blushing captive. I stumble backward, my head spinning, but his strong arm holds me in place.

Clouds drift away from the full moon, drenching the road in silver light. The oak trees' twisted branches loom overhead, forming a skeletal canopy.

Dread coils around my neck like the hangman's noose.

Any notion that the horseman might be a psycho in a costume vanishes under the overwhelming evidence. The legend of Sixteen String Jack is true.

How on earth am I going to impress a supernatural being with a burning pumpkin for a head? He's probably had hundreds of women over the years, and won't get excited over a newly unemployed secretary.

Jack's deep growl makes my hair stand on end and chases away my insecurities.

It's too late to worry about my lack of skills. It's also too late to consider that the creature beneath the pumpkin head and antique clothes is a ghost that just turned solid.

He's given me a chance to live, and I intend to survive long enough to teach William a lesson.

"Well then?" he says, his voice unusually husky for a man with no head. "Will you accept my challenge?"

My fingers tremble over his thick length.

Could I get away with giving him a handjob over his breeches?

As I stroke up and down his shaft, it lengthens and thickens to the point where every ridge, every vein, every contour protrudes through the silk fabric.

Right now, standing tucked beneath his shoulder with my gaze pointed to the floor, I could be with anyone. It almost feels like I'm cheating with a bigger, better man than William.

The pulse between my legs pounds so hard that I have to squeeze my thighs together to muffle the sound.

Fuck.

He's twice the size of my ex and three times as thick.

I slide my fingers over the ridge of his cockhead and stifle a moan as heat floods my pussy. This guy has some serious potential.

"Take it out," he rasps.

He doesn't need to tell me twice.

I fumble around his fly, finding a flap of fabric that runs diagonally over his crotch. After undoing the buckle at the top, I slip my hand inside.

His flesh is warmer than expected, with soft pubic hair that curls around my fingers like vines. His chest rumbles, and I delve further down and wrap my fingers around a thick and hot pulsing length.

The horseman groans.

So do I.

It's the longest, meatiest cock, adorned with prominent

veins and a bulbous head. A bead of precum glistens on its tip, making me gulp.

"Well?" he says, his deep voice sharp with impatience.

I lick my lips and run my hand along the shaft. "It's just so..."

"Were you expecting a summer squash?"

"Of course not," I blurt. "But I've never seen anything so huge."

At the horseman's rusty chuckle, the rope of tension around my neck eases, and I can finally exhale.

"I'll wager you've never tasted anything so hearty. I'm standing. It's your turn to deliver."

He has a point, and he's been unusually patient.

I drop to my knees, my palms trailing down his body for balance. The fabric of his cloak is warm for a specter, and the ground beneath my shins is as spongy as moss.

It's impossible to know where to look—at the oversized pumpkin or the oversized cock, which fills the entire right side of my periphery.

"Having second thoughts?" he rumbles.

I gulp, my gaze landing on the blade of his ax. My dilemma should be simple: lose my head to this homicidal specter or suck his monstrous cock. Even that second option is perilous—his erection is alarmingly big. It could cut off my air and send me to an early grave.

He clears his throat with a hollow sound that stiffens my spine.

My gaze jerks back to his cock. It's surprisingly alive up close and flushed with prominent veins running down its underside. I try not to imagine how it would feel, splitting me open, but my pussy clenches with need.

Jack grunts, sounding like his patience is wearing thin.

I choke out the words, "No second thoughts. I'm ready."

He pulls back the fabric of his cloak with the hand not holding the ax. I lean forward and place a kiss on his damp cockhead. Apart from being almost twice the size of William's dick, it's no different from a living penis.

I run my tongue up the length of his shaft. He smells mostly of stone, if such a thing is possible, with the taste of human skin.

Jack's breathy groan fills my pussy with a thrill of satisfaction. I reach into his breeches to cup his balls, but he grabs my wrist.

"Time's a-wastin'," he growls.

Pushing aside the question of why he wants to keep me away from his testicles, I wrap my fingers around his erection and squeeze. Jack moans as I flick my tongue back and forth over his slit and lavish his shaft with up and down strokes.

An owl hoots in the distance and a cool breeze blows overhead.

Time to get to work.

I part my lips and engulf Jack's cock in my mouth. My jaw opens to its full capacity to accommodate his size, and I hum my appreciation.

"Wanton wench," he says, his voice breathy. "You sure like the taste of my cock."

Sucking in my cheeks to create more of a vacuum, I hide a smile. It's too early to celebrate. I still have to make him cum. As Jack rocks forward on the balls of his feet, I ease him further into my mouth.

He's astonishingly docile, considering he wanted to chop off my head, but all men become tame with their cocks in another's mouth.

Timing the movements of my head with the up-and-down strokes of my hands on his cock, I build up a rhythm that makes Jack pant. He breathes heavier than a normal man, his chest sounding like bellows.

Heat builds low in my belly and the pulse between my legs quickens. Wetness floods my pussy, and my clit throbs for attention. I squeeze my thighs together to create some friction.

Maybe it's the outdoors, maybe it's the danger, maybe it's the thought that I'm already on the rebound from William, but I've never felt sexier or more alive.

My eyelids flutter shut, and I picture myself at the back of an eighteenth-century tavern, sucking off a handsome highwayman.

"Eyes on me," he growls.

I tilt up my head and meet the triangular holes in his pumpkin, filled with flames.

My stomach drops. It's a jumping-off-the-dive-board sensation that makes me inhale in a sharp breath. Jack's substitute head was huge when I was standing, but kneeling here with his cock in my mouth makes him look otherworldly.

It doesn't help that he's still holding that fucking ax.

"Good girl," he snarls.

My heartbeat quickens, and I hum around my mouthful. I really shouldn't be getting so excited over a malevolent spirit's praise.

"You like that?" he says without moving the pumpkin's carved maw. "You like sucking the cock of a vengeful ghost?"

I choke around his cock.

Since when could ghosts materialize body parts for sexual gratification? Then again, what the hell do I know?

"More?" he asks. "A lusty lass like you can take it."

His words send a bolt of arousal straight to my pussy.

My hand drifts between my legs, and I rub my clit through my petticoat, apron, and skirt.

Chuckling, Jack cups the back of my head with a gloved hand. This time, warmth radiates through the leather. Before I can consider this temperature change, his cockhead hits the back of my throat.

My pussy tightens, wishing it was the one taking such a heavy dick.

"Here it comes." He pushes forward, toward my tonsils, somehow circumventing my gag reflex.

Every time William used to go deep, I would retch and splutter. It's different with Jack. My throat relaxes, accommodating his cockhead. Perhaps deep down, my body knew William wasn't the one.

Jack pushes forward, filling me so deeply that my eyes water, and I stop taking in air. My lungs burn, and the edges of my vision fill with spots. As though sensing I'm in danger of fainting, Jack pulls back a fraction of an inch, easing the tension.

"Take deep breaths." He runs his fingers through my hair, the caresses a balm on my frantic heart.

My brows rise. Is the headless horseman being considerate? Now's probably not the time to question his motives.

"Alright," I try to say around his girth, but the words are muffled.

I inhale through my nostrils, filling my lungs with air. Once I've gotten used to his size, I give him a nod.

He pulls back several inches until his tip stretches my lips. I flick my tongue up and down its slit and lap up the salty precum.

"You are taking my cock so well," he rumbles.

I preen at his praise.

Jack snaps his hips and reenters me with a sharp thrust that sends shocks to the marrow of my bones. He pulls out again as I swallow around him, only to fuck into me once more.

I should cough, I should splutter, I should struggle for air, but my pussy is so hot and wet and slick that all I care about is my release. It's impossible to reach my bare clit, since I'm kneeling on my skirts, so I rub harder through the layers of fabric.

Up and down, up and down, I move my fingers in time with Jack's thrusts. Pleasure circles my core like a cobra, coiling and collecting until I can't stand the pressure.

I need more friction.

My ears fill with Jack's heavy breaths and deep, shuddering groans. I lash my tongue from side to side, wondering if I'll survive the night.

"Good girl."

Flames coil from the pumpkin's jagged maw, but the words echo from deep within his belly. I keep my eyes upward, just as he ordered, even though my vision blurs.

"Such an eager slut." His fingers tighten around the back of my head. "But I wager you could take even more."

I make a noise in the back of my throat and try to nod through his iron grip. This is no longer about impressing Jack. I want this for myself. Bobbing forward as much as he'll allow, I encourage him to give it to me harder, faster, thicker.

Jack pistons in and out of my mouth, his breath quickening. The flames that fill the pumpkin's eye-holes burn so bright that my vision fills with yellow.

I rub the fabric over my clit, my pussy pulsing with need. As Jack's moans become deeper, more guttural, more inhuman, every nerve in my body thrums with anticipation.

The air stills, and the flames that fill his eye holes recede. My skin tingles, the way it does when waiting for lightning to strike after thunder. The drumbeat between my ears beats loud enough to muffle the sound of his movements.

Jack is about to cum, and all I can think about is how I'll swallow all his spunk.

His cock swells and a roar fills my ears that rattles my skull and hits every inch of my skin like static. The cock in my mouth pulses, once, twice, three times, before he pulls out with a satisfied groan.

I sit back on my heels and frown. Where's the cum? Do ghosts have dry orgasms? Part of me wanted a mouthful of jism.

Jack tucks himself back into his breeches with one hand. The other holds the ax up to the sky. Moonlight glints on its sharp edge, and I swear it's already coated with blood.

Fucking hell.

What if he cuts off my head so I can provide him with an eternity of blowjobs?

It's time to remind him of our bargain.

"Didn't I impress you?" My voice trembles.

With a deep chortle, he offers me his hand. I take that as a good sign and let him help me to my feet.

"You are free to go, Milady, but I would like to make you one more offer."

"What?"

"Satisfy me until sunrise, and I will show you the location of five hundred gold sovereigns."

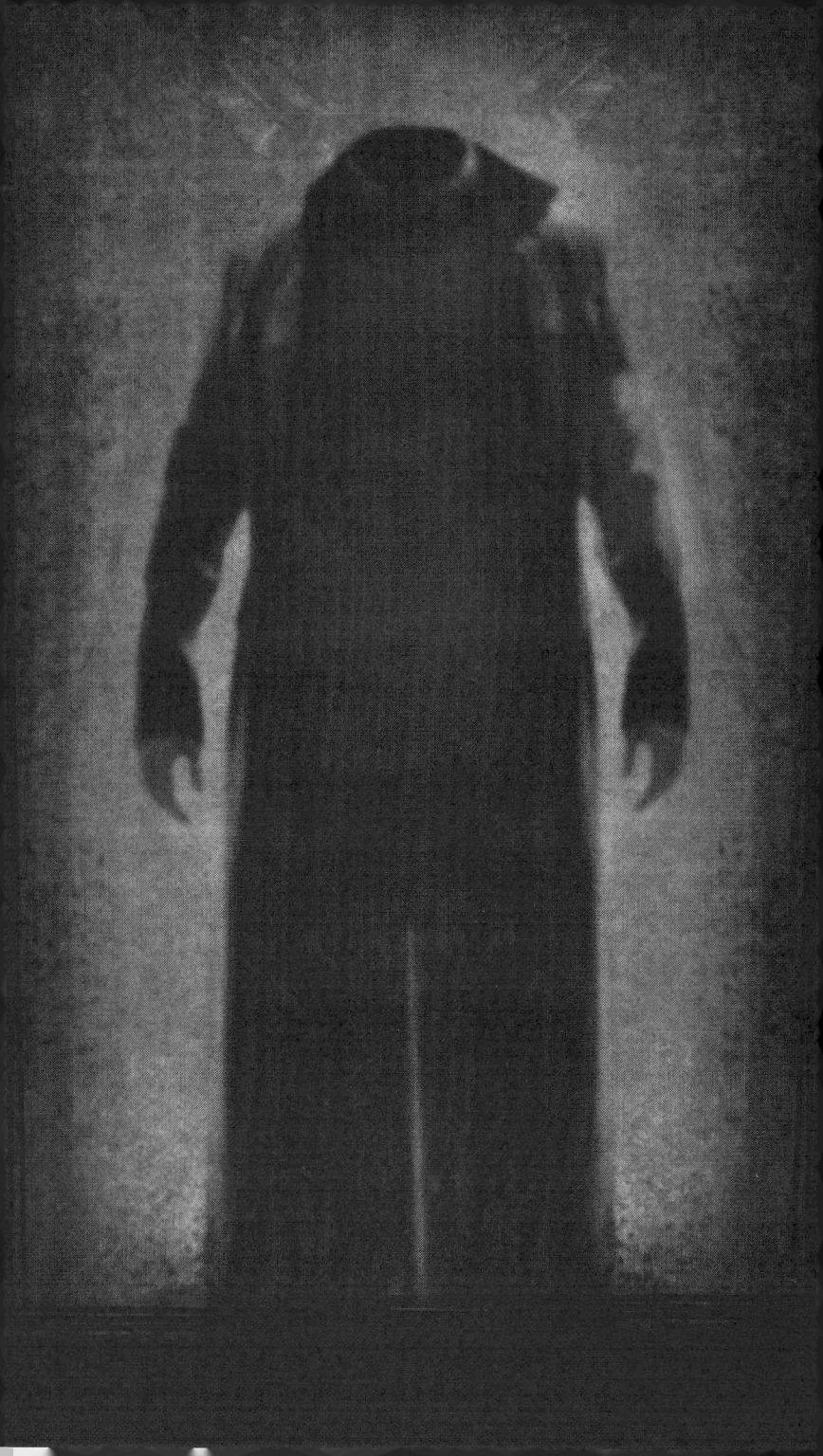

Chapter Four

I shuffle on my feet, snapping the stitches of my petticoat. My mind makes rapid-fire calculations. William once purchased a gold sovereign for £5,000.

Jack glowers down at me through triangular eye-holes that look like gateways to the hottest pits of hell. He stands so close that supernatural evil hits my skin like sparks.

He's waiting for my answer to his indecent proposal.

Sex in exchange for over two million pounds worth of gold.

Propriety says I should make my excuses and leave. Common sense says I should return to what's left of my car and drive it back into civilization.

Jack lowers his other arm, letting the blade of his ax hit the cobblestones with a clank and a shower of sparks. My heart leaps into my throat. That has to be a good sign, right?

"Your answer?" he snarls.

"May I ask a few questions?"

He nods.

"You asked me to satisfy you." I gulp. "Will it hurt?"

Jack pauses for a few heartbeats before answering, "Only in the most delicious way."

Heat surges between my legs. I already know from the ache in my throat that fucking his cock would be phenomenal. But what if sex with a specter is deadly?

"Will I come out of it alive?" I ask.

Jack cups my cheek. It's a gesture so tender that my breath catches. Warmth radiates through the butter-soft leather glove, making my skin tingle. The affection causes the butterflies in my stomach to flutter their wings.

"If you accept this second challenge, you will end the night as a very rich woman."

I do not doubt that. Sixteen String Jack was a legendary highwayman who robbed Princess Amelia and the Bank of England's governor.

A fraction of Jack's stolen gold would finance my new home and pay for a lawyer to defend me against William's attempts at revenge. But what if I can't satisfy Jack?

"And if I fail?" I ask.

Jack shakes his pumpkin head. "If your cunt is as sweet as your mouth, you will be worth every pound of that treasure."

My throat tightens. "But that doesn't answer—"

Jack places a finger over my lips, cutting off my words. "You will come to no harm. On my honor as a gentleman and a thief."

Biting down on my bottom lip, I squeeze my eyes shut. Should I believe him? A moment ago, he wanted me dead. But what are my options?

Thanks to William, I'm jobless, homeless, and potentially going to be arrested for stealing a company car. If my ex goes ahead with those threats, it will take weeks, if not months, to repair my reputation, and then what?

My future was tied up with Willian and Whitechapel

Finance—it's all I've ever known. But one night of sex with a long-dead highwayman could give me a life of financial independence.

"What do I need to do?"

"Look at me," he says.

My eyes snap open. I hope to every imaginable deity that Jack doesn't demand a kiss. The flames curling from the pumpkin's jagged maw look like they could sear my soul to cinders.

"For the rest of All Hallows Eve, you will submit to my desires," he rumbles. "You will give me free rein of your cunt and mouth and rump. Should you wish to end proceedings, you will leave empty-handed."

In other words, he wants to fill my holes.

"Alright," I whisper.

Jack scoops me into his arms and stalks toward my sliced-open Beetle. His demonic horse backs away, glaring at us through eyes that burn hotter than hellfire.

I clutch at Jack's cloak and whisper, "Where are we going?"

"Not far," he rumbles.

Before I can ask for more details, he swings his ax across the air, sending shards of glass flying into the trees that border the road. Then he lowers me onto the hood of my car.

He looms over me, his monstrous pumpkin the only source of light.

"Jack?" I croak.

"Lift your skirts," he says, his voice a rough command.

My clit throbs as I gather the lower half of my dress and petticoat over my hips. A cool breeze blows over my exposed thighs, making the skin there tighten into goosebumps.

"Push your drawers to one side."

It takes a second to register that he's referring to my knickers.

As I expose my pussy, the lace trim brushes over my clit. My breath catches, and the muscles of my core clench. I need more friction.

Jack draws so closely that I tremble at the heat of his flames.

"My, my, what a comely little cunt."

My clit swells at his praise. And my gaze wanders down to the erection straining his silk breeches. The hours would fly past if I could get Jack to pleasure me with that meaty cock.

"Thank you," I murmur.

"You should see how prettily you glisten."

I tilt my hips toward his pumpkin. "Are you just going to look at it?"

Jack's arm shoots out like a cobra and grabs my neck, shattering any semblance of security. His touch is firm but not tight, although he could cut off my air with a squeeze of those large fingers.

Shit.

Did I really have to challenge a murderous ghoul?

An apology bubbles up to the back of my throat, but my lips can't form the words.

Jack leans over me, bringing his head so close to mine that I hear the snap and crackle of his flames. Sweat gathers on my brow, and I force my gaze away from his eyeholes.

"What do you want, wench?" he snarls.

I reach down between our bodies, trying to palm his erection, but he presses down on my hips so it lies flush against my pussy. Jack isn't going to fall for that trick again.

"Answer me," he hisses.

"Y-your cock," the words come out garbled.

"What about it?"

"Please fuck me with that huge, thick erection," I blurt.

He loosens his grip on my neck and draws back a few inches. "You will earn that privilege."

My brow furrows. "How?"

"You will take Rudger."

Dread pools in my gut, which tightens with a sense of impending terror. I glance over his shoulder at the horse and grimace. No amount of treasure could make me stoop to something so depraved.

"Absolutely not." I place my hands on his shoulders and give him a shove, but he's immovable.

I wait for Jack to explode with rage, the way William might in the face of rejection, but he snickers. The sound is breathy, joyful, yet oddly sinister. He's taking my refusal rather well.

"Rudger is the weapon I stole from His Majesty's executioner," he says.

Some of the tension eases, and I relax back onto the hood of my car. "Um... What is it?"

His ax spins in his palm, its blade glinting in the moonlight, before Jack points the hilt toward my pussy. "This is Rudger."

"Oh."

An inanimate object is a hundred times better than a horse, but do I want to be fucked with his murder weapon?

Five hundred gold sovereigns say yes.

"What say you, wench? Will you take its haft?"

"Alright," I say, assuming that haft is old English for a handle.

Jack spins the ax once more, with the blade pointing toward my neck. I suck in a sharp breath. He won't kill me —he promised. He needs me alive to satisfy his needs.

He runs the flat of the ax's blade over my cleavage,

making me whimper. The blade is smooth and cool on my fevered flesh but does nothing to lower my temperature.

Blood roars between my ears, and rapid, shallow breaths whistle from between my clenched teeth. One false move and he'll snick an artery.

"Frightened?" he asks.

"A little," I whisper.

With a flick of my wrist, he slices through the fabric of my blouse, exposing my left breast.

"Beautiful," he says, his voice warm.

The words send a shiver of pleasure across my skin, but I don't dare make a move to thank him in case I ruin his concentration.

Jack makes the same sharp movement on my right side before hovering the blade over my corset. I clench my teeth, hoping he won't try to slice through something so tightly attached to my ribs.

He runs the ax over the top of one exposed leg then slices my skirt and petticoat into ribbons. I shiver as the fabric slides down my skin and gathers across my car's hood.

My pulse quickens to a drumroll. Am I seriously going to let him fuck me with the handle of that ax?

"Your cunt is aching for my Rudger," he growls, the flames in his nostrils receding. "I can smell it."

I bite back a moan as he slides the blade up my inner thigh, my muscles clenching in anticipation.

Jack grabs my knee with his free hand, pushing it further apart from the other and laying me bare. A cool breeze meanders over my exposed pussy, sending shudders down my spine.

This is edgier than anything I ever did with William— no one's ever wanted to penetrate me with an ax.

Ax.

Ax as in ax murderer.

Just as the wood brushes my outer lips, I blurt, "Wait!"

Jack pauses. It's hard to tell what he's thinking with a face carved out of a pumpkin, but I need to know one thing.

"That's the same ax you use to chop off heads." This is a statement, not a question because there's no way a monster like Sixteen String Jack would keep a spare one just for the ladies.

The flames that fill the pumpkin's eye-holes narrow. "What of it?"

"You can't put that thing inside me without cleaning it."

My heart stills as I await his response, and I close my thighs. Surely Jack won't decapitate me for asking for the bare minimum?

With a harrumph, he dips the entire handle into his fiery maw, filling the air with the scent of burning firewood. When he extracts the ax, it's shiny and new.

"Better?" he asks, his voice sharp.

"Perfect." My legs flop open. "Now, fuck me with Rudger."

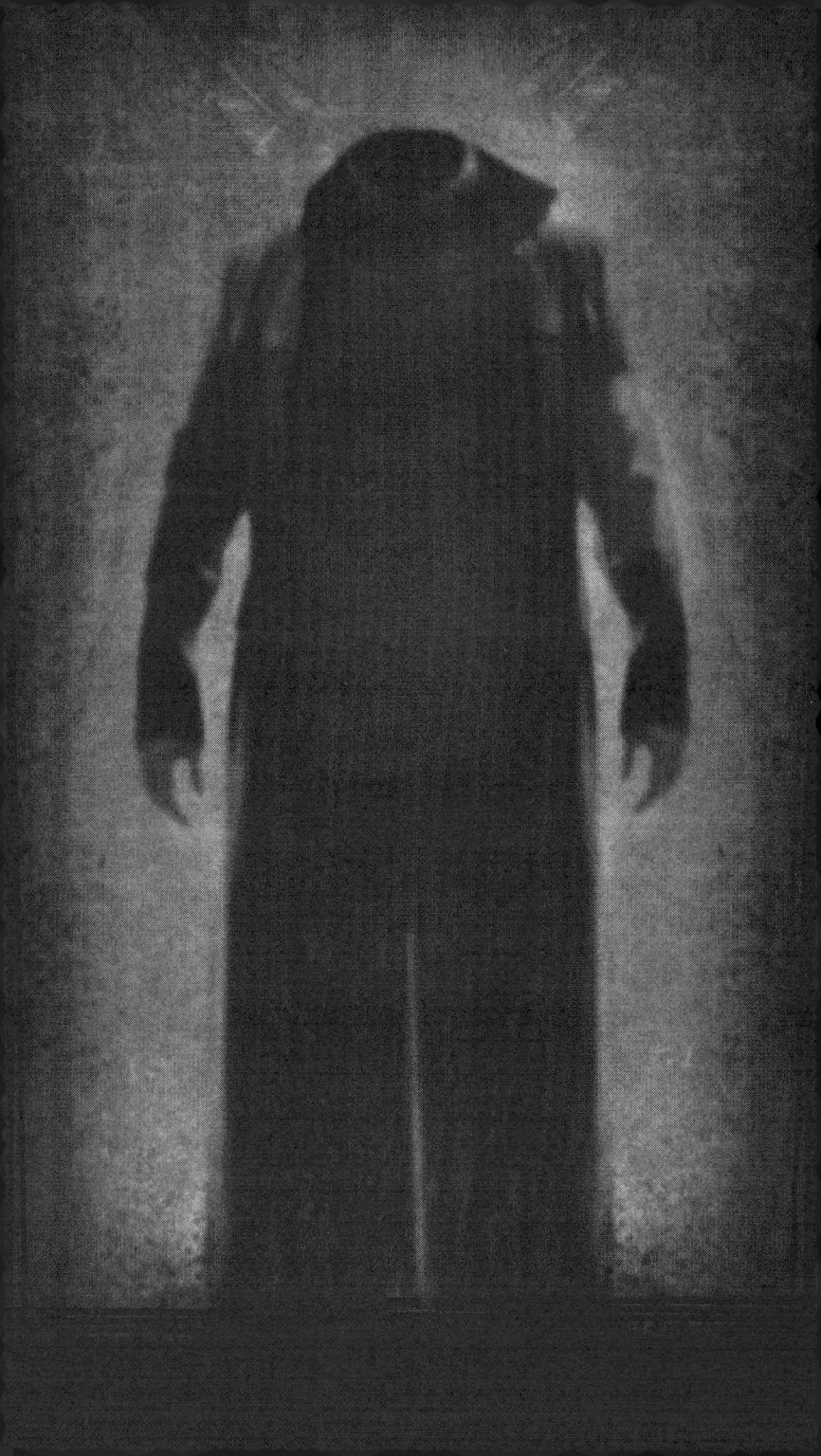

Chapter Five

I lie back on the hood of my car splaying my legs open, with Jack circling my clit with the knob at the end of his ax's handle. The wood provides delicious friction against my sensitive flesh and sends heat flaring across my pussy.

Sucking my lips into my mouth, I suppress a moan.

"No," Jack says, his voice echoing like thunder. "I want to hear your pleasure."

"Okay," I whisper.

He slides the ax's handle to my entrance, drenching it in my fluids.

I arch my back and groan.

"Good girl," he rumbles. "You are so eager and wet."

Without further warning, he plunges the handle of his ax into my pussy.

It's thicker than I expected and still retaining the heat of his flames. I cry out, my thighs trying to slam closed, but Jack holds me open with a gloved hand.

"That's it," he says in a voice that booms through my skull. "Take the heft like a good little strumpet."

An ache shoots through my pussy that makes me pant harder than his horse. My pelvic muscles clench and spasm around the thick cylinder of wood, trying to adjust to its girth.

Just as I'm catching my breath, Jack gives the ax another gentle push.

Fuck.

I'm so full that I feel it in the back of my throat.

"Oh," I groan. "Too much."

"You will take what you are given and be thankful," he roars.

Jack pulls out the ax, leaving my pussy closing around the emptiness, trying to hold it in. He shoves the handle back in again, making me gasp.

"F-f-f-fuck," I hiss.

"You love it." He yanks it out.

I do, but it's difficult to admit. Less than an hour ago, I was raging at William because he wanted me to suck off his uncles. Now, I'm lying naked on the hood of my car, letting an evil phantom fuck me with his murder weapon.

Jack pumps the handle in and out of my pussy, filling me, stretching me, making me squirm. He clutches my knee as though he's afraid I might escape, but I'm so slippery and wet, and the handle feels so good, that I never want it to end.

"Look at you," he growls. "Taking my executioner's ax like a penny slattern."

Is this some kind of eighteenth-century degradation kink?

"S-surely I'm worth at least a shilling?" I say with a whimper.

He roars with laughter. "Sixpence and not a ha'penny more!"

My cheeks turn hot, but it's nothing compared to the furnace he's stoking in my core. Why the hell is this talk turning me on? I should be displeased, not delighted. I sling an arm over my face and groan.

"Wench," Jack growls and quickens his pace.

"Yes?" I say with a shudder.

"Show your face. I want to see you melt."

My arm flops to the side, and I stare into his pumpkin's eye holes.

Jack draws closer and runs his leathery hand up and down my thigh, sending tingles across my skin.

"Good girl," he mumbles. "See how well you're taking the ax. Your cunt was made for fucking."

I swallow back a whimper.

Jack continues sliding the handle in and out of my pussy, whispering words that make my toes curl. "I have waited centuries to find a hussy who could take my wood," he growls. "You're a special little slut."

My nipples tingle, begging to be sucked. My clit swells with his filthy words. It turns out that I don't mind being treated with disrespect as long as it's with my consent.

Pressure builds low in my belly, making my nerves burn hotter than Jack's flames. Without meaning to, I buck my hips in counterpoint to the movements of his ax. Sparks of rapture detonate in delicious pathways up my belly and along my inner thighs. I've never been fucked so thoroughly.

"That's it," he growls. "Show me that you're worthy of my cock."

A cry catches in my throat. I move faster, my eyes watering with Jack's heavy thrusts. There's a subtle knot on the wooden shaft, which rubs over a spot inside me that floods my pussy with molten ecstasy.

I circle my hips, making sure to hit that spot over and over and over until the pressure makes me implode.

An orgasm hits me so hard that I tumble backward onto the car's hood, clenching and spasming around the handle's shaft. Jack pumps it in and out, without mercy or restraint, riding out my climax until I scream.

I've never come so hard or with so much noise.

He pulls out the ax, leans into me, and murmurs into my ear, "How prettily you shriek, but I think you can go louder."

"What..." I inhale a shaky breath. "What do you mean?"

Jack flips me over, so I'm lying face-down on the trunk. Above us, clouds drift away from the moon, drenching me in light.

Before I can even take in the sight of the sliced-in-half car and all the glass littered across the road, he hooks his hands beneath my hips and pulls me onto my hands and knees.

"Jack," I stutter. "What are you doing?"

"Are you ready for more?"

I lick my lips, my pussy tingling at the prospect of being fucked doggy-style with that cock. After taking the handle of his ax so well, I deserve a reward.

"Well?" he says without a trace of impatience.

"Please," I rasp.

"Here they come."

They?

I glance over my shoulder, expecting to find Jack stroking his erection and maybe holding his ax. The undead bastard is wielding two antique pistols.

"What's that?" I tumble onto my ass, my mouth falling agape.

Jack studies the firearm in his left hand. "Do you like them?"

My mouth opens and closes. "Um..."

"The double-barrel, flintlock horse pistols I used on the highways."

My gaze drops to its metallic barrels. I'm no expert on

guns, but I handled the paperwork for William's purchase of a 1770 flintlock pistol. It was rumored to belong to Dick Turpin and sold at auction for £40,000.

"Are they loaded?"

"Fuck them and see," he replies with a rattling laugh.

I bite down on the inside of my cheek and force myself to remember that he gave me his word as a gentleman to do me no harm.

"Are they included as my reward for satisfying you tonight?" I ask.

"If you can take them, they're yours."

I gulp. It's almost a shame to ruin such valuable antiques. "Alright," I say with a shiver and move onto my hands and knees. "Clean them, and we have a deal."

Jack's booming laughter fills my chest with warmth. "You're a brave little wench." He slaps my ass with a gloved hand. "My guns are yours, but only if you can take them both."

Anticipation skitters down my spine. I push out my ass, relax my muscles, and gaze over my shoulder as he dips the pistols into his fire.

"You are a glorious sight." His deep voice resonates across my bare back. "Two plump cheeks surrounding a dripping cunt."

"Please," I whisper.

One of the pistol's barrels makes a slow trail up my inner thigh, sending skitters across my skin. I'm breathing so shallow and fast that my vision fills with dancing dots. As the cool metal grazes my outer lips, I moan.

Jack sides the barrel of the pistol into my pussy, giving my muscles a heartbeat to close around it before it moves with slow, shallow strokes.

"Deeper," I murmur.

"Not yet." A light spank lands on my ass, cushioned by his soft leather glove.

"Why?"

"This one is meant to get wet."

It takes a moment to understand that he plans to stick it in my ass. That, and the leathery thumb circling my pucker. My pulse kicks up a notch, and my pussy floods with more heat.

Jack shoves out my thighs with his forearm, making me spread my legs wider. I lean forward, resting my weight on my elbows and chest. Right now, it feels like I'm on display.

I'm so wet that fluids spill down my inner thighs. So wet that the metal pistol slides all the way down my channel until its trigger guard nestles flush against my swollen clit. As the gun's hammer lies flat against my asshole, I clench around the barrel.

"Oh," I say with a breathy moan. "That feels so good."

"Wait until I start fucking you with them in earnest," he says with a filthy laugh and pulls the first pistol out of my pussy. "Good girl. You've got it nice and wet."

My asshole trembles.

Jack eases my pucker open with a finger and thumb before resting the pistol's muzzle between my asscheeks. It's about that time that I register that his pistol is double-barreled.

"Oh, fuck," I whisper. "It's going to be too big."

"Easy now."

Warm fluid spills at the base of my spine, just before the cleft of my ass. It trickles down my crease, toward my hole. My nostrils fill with the mingled scents of cinnamon, cloves, nutmeg, and ginger.

A giggle fills my chest. "Is that pumpkin spice?"

"Shhh" He pushes the cooling liquid to my asshole. "This will help you take both barrels."

I tell myself it's a pumpkin-based lubricant, and not a diabolical form of ectoplasm, even though the substance slides over my sphincter like a salve. Through some measure of sorcery, those muscles loosen, and Jack slides the pistol inside.

"Oh, fuck."

My thighs tremble at the stretch. The gun is already lubricated with my juices, so there's only a slight amount of friction, but I tighten and tremble around the double barrels.

"Wonderful," Jack says, his voice hoarse. "I knew you could accommodate my pistol. Now, let's see how well you can handle two."

He slides the second one into my pussy, setting the nerves around there alight. I'm so full that I can barely breathe.

"Now, take them!" Jack roars.

He pulls out the pistol in my pussy, only to thrust the one in my ass as far as it can go. I fall forward onto my face, exhaling the contents of my lungs with a low moan.

The double cylinders take turns pushing, pulling, stretching. I cling onto what's left of the windscreen wipers and pant.

Throughout Jack's pummeling, my ears ring with his maniacal laugh. The sound is as loud as bellows, as though it's coming from the depths of hell. I'd find it alarming if I didn't have two huge metal cylinders pistoning in and out of my ass and pussy. Perhaps even horrifying if it wasn't the soundtrack to an even more powerful orgasm.

Jack doesn't slow, doesn't pause, doesn't tire, doesn't stop. All I can do is kneel on the hood with my head on its metal surface and take the pistol fucking.

I don't know if this next climax will kill me or blow me to bits, either one would be worth the consequences.

"You should see how my flintlocks are stretching your holes," he says with a demonic cackle. "By the time I've finished, you will hunger for no other man but me!"

Before I can consider what he means, a second climax explodes through me like gunfire. Dynamite sizzles across every nerve, making my limbs tremble. Tremors wrack my body, tearing me into splinters. My eyes roll to the back of my head, and I open my mouth in a silent scream.

The siren of a police car penetrates the haze, bringing with it the distant flare of red and blue lights. I raise my head and frown. Did William already convince the police to come after me for taking the company car?

"Bloody hellfire," Jack mutters. "The magic here wears thin."

With an annoyed grunt, he pulls the pistols out of my ass and pussy, leaving me empty and clenching.

"Let us move proceedings to my hideout."

Chapter Six

I'm still panting and trembling when Jack helps me off the hood of my car and sets me on my feet. My knees give way, and I fall forward, only for him to hold me steady with an arm around my waist.

Sirens penetrate the fog, bringing in a glimpse of the real world. Jack snaps his fingers, and an instant later, I'm staring into the fiery eyes of his hellhorse.

A chill settles over my skin, and I suppress a shiver.

"Cold?" he asks.

I shake my head, not wanting to share the warmth of his flames.

Jack drapes his cloak over my shoulders.

"But I'm not—"

"You are naked." He scoops me into his arms. "I would kill those bastards before they lay their eyes upon what's mine."

The butterflies in my stomach preen at the implied praise. However, the part of me that's used to summarizing William's correspondence wonders if he's changed his mind about our arrangement and plans on dragging me to hell.

"But you said you'll set me free."

"Aye." He lifts me off my feet and cradles me to his broad chest. "But you belong to me until the first rays of sunshine."

I rest my head against his shoulder and exhale a breath of relief. With his free hand, Jack grabs the horse's smoky mane and mounts it while I glance around for signs of the approaching police.

The horse gallops through the smog, leaving the sirens fading in the distance. Jack adjusts me so I'm sitting astride his mount, with his erection nestled between my ass cheeks.

I feel the ridge of his cockhead through the layers of fabric, and my pussy surges with renewed heat. My clit pulses and swells in temp with the hoofbeats, and my head spins.

Whatever magic is animating Jack seems to have a strange effect on my libido. I should be frightened, even scandalized at what I've done with a dead man, but my body wants more.

I'm still aching from the ax handle and the pistols, but a greedy part of me still needs that juicy cock. Leaning against his broad chest, I run a hand up and down his silk-covered thigh and ask, "Where are we going?"

"Back to my old haunt, where we can have some real fun."

"Are you going to fuck me anytime soon?"

Jack's bellowing laugh reverberates against my back. "You are as lovely as you are lustful, but there's a time and a place."

"But—"

His large hand cups my pussy.

I grab his muscular thighs and gasp.

"Greedy girl," he growls and presses down on my clit

with a leathery finger. "Be patient, and I will give you more cock than you can handle."

"Yes," I murmur.

The horse races through the fog, passing tall, twisted trees whose branches create a chilling canopy. Jack's erection lies so nestled in the cleft of my ass that I can feel its every ridge.

But none of that matters with his leathery finger teasing my clit. Tight, slow circles explore my swollen bundle of nerves, making my pussy throb with slippery heat.

"What is your name?" he asks, his fiery breath warming the back of my neck.

My chest rises and falls with shallow breaths, and I whisper, "Bess."

"Do you like that, Beautiful Bess?"

I bite down on my bottom lip and suppress a moan.

Jack pinches my clit between his thick fingers, shocking me with a jolt of arousal. "Never hide your pleasure from me, Wench. I want to hear your screams."

"A-alright," I rasp.

His finger travels lower towards the wetness at my opening, and he growls his approval. "You're slick for me."

"Yes," I say with a groan.

"You moan so prettily, but you can do better than that." The edge of his thumb makes lazy strokes up and down my swollen clit. "Come on, Bess. Louder."

His thumb rubs harder and the horse's movements press Jack's erection deeper into my ass crease. I clench around his shaft, causing him to moan. Jack pulls me tighter, making rhythmic thrusts.

Sweat breaks out across my skin. My thighs spasm. I throw my head back, my breath hitching. "More."

Jack's thumb strokes my clit harder, faster, while his finger pushes into my pussy.

"I wish I could kiss the creamy skin on your neck," he rumbles and quickens his pace. "I wish I could taste your sweet cunt."

With his other hand, he rolls my nipple between his fingers, alternating between gentle tugs and pinches. This is more pleasure than a woman can bear. I circle my hips, adding to the friction.

Jack's finger delves in and out, barely skimming the spot that fills me with fireworks. I wriggle about, trying to climax, but each time I get close, he pulls out.

"Stop teasing," I whisper, my pussy spasming and clenching, desperate for another orgasm. "More."

"None of that," he growls. "You will take what I give you and be satisfied."

I'm so painfully aroused that my brain can't process why he's withholding his cock. Perhaps Jack wants to hear me beg.

"Please," I croak.

"Please, what?" he asks, his voice filled with warmth. "Tell me what you need."

"I need you to fuck me from behind with that monstrous dick. I need you to pound into me until I see stars."

His malicious laugh makes my hair stand on end. "What else?"

"I need you to make me cum."

"Very well," he rumbles. "You will get that and more, but you must agree to another condition."

"What's that?"

The horse slows to a canter, and as the mist recedes, it walks into the stable yard that backs onto Whitechapel Cemetery. I've passed this place several times while visiting the graves of William's parents, but this is the first time I've been inside.

Jack gathers me in his arms again and dismounts, leaving his horse to trot into one of the stalls.

"What's the condition?" I clutch his shoulder. "Where are we going?"

"Somewhere private to prepare you for a long, hard ride."

I clench the muscles of my pussy. "But I'm already wet."

A belly laugh rumbles from deep within the pumpkin, making his chest vibrate. I cling to the lapels of his jacket, my gaze darting around the stable yard.

"What's so funny?"

"Wait and see."

My eyes narrow. "Are you this mysterious with all the girls or just me?"

Jack pauses. "I haven't had a woman since I was alive. Haven't wanted one until now."

"Why?"

"It's been centuries since anyone has caught my interest," he replies. "There's a way about you I find impossible to resist."

All the breath escapes my lungs, and my mouth goes unusually dry. Jack saw something in me that William didn't. That's something I'm unlikely to forget.

"How about you?" he rumbles. "Do you make a habit of grabbing strange men's cocks?"

"Only yours."

With a satisfied grunt, he carries me into the next stall, which is smaller, warmer, and candle-lit. Leather saddles and bridles hang on the walls, making the space look more like a tack room.

After he sets me on my feet, I turn in a slow circle, taking in an array of leather equipment. There are halters, harnesses, and heavy plumes, but the equipment is far too small for a horse.

Everything's more fitting to a much smaller equine or even a human—

"What's this?" I ask.

Jack sweeps his arm toward a picture on the wall. I walk to it, my jaw dropping.

Staring out from behind the yellowing parchment is the drawing of a woman trussed up like a show horse, complete with a leather saddle on her back.

My jaw drops. I whirl around to meet Jack's fiery gaze. "You want me to wear a bit and bridle?"

He closes the distance between us, standing so close that his flames flicker against my skin. His chest heaves, and his breath quickens. "I want to train you like a show pony. I want to ride you so hard that you neigh for more. Any objections?"

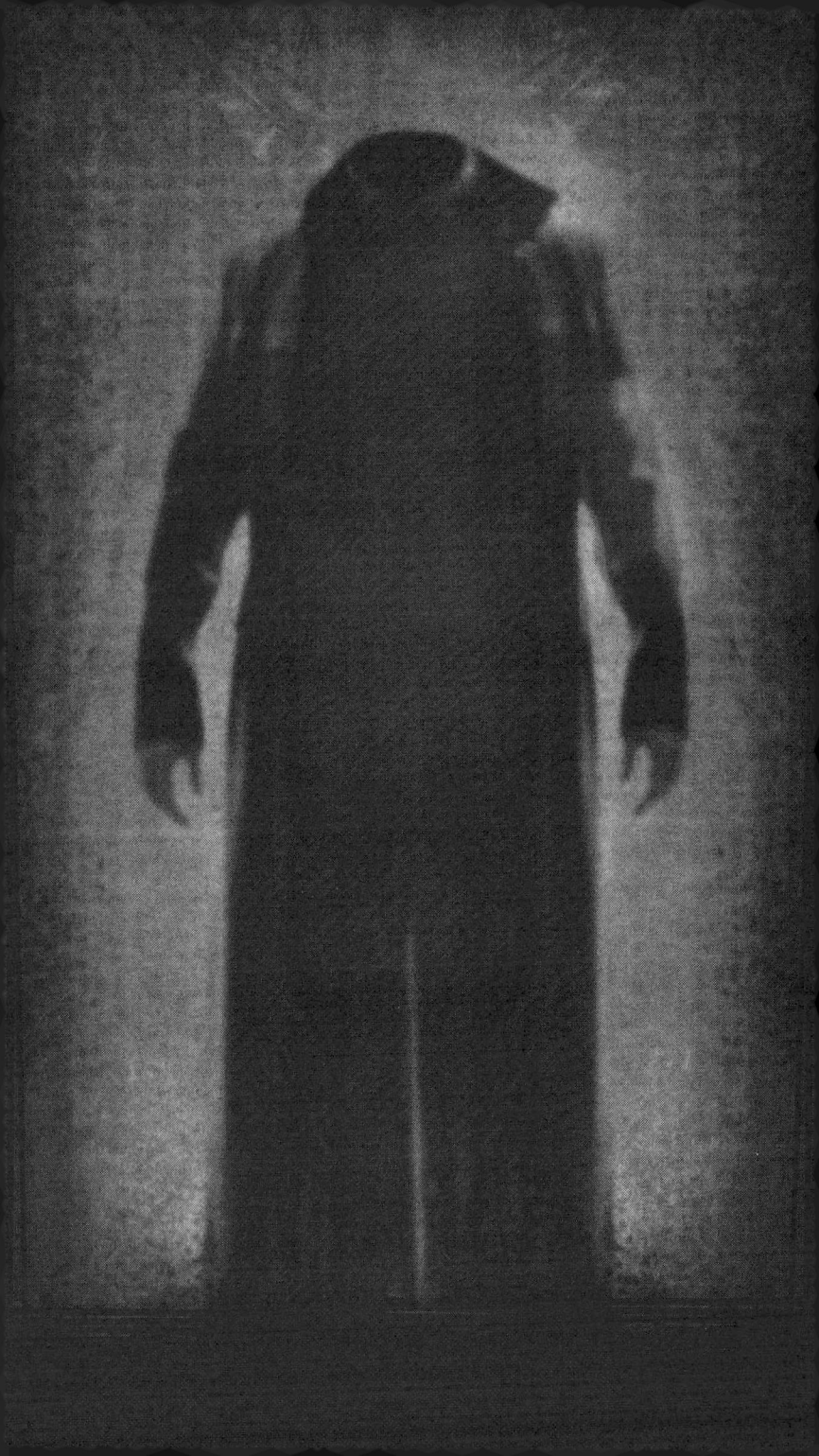

Chapter Seven

I can't believe a headless highwayman has aroused me to a point beyond reason. This has to be some trick of black magic. How else can I explain getting hot at the thought of becoming his pony girl?

Candlelight warms the stable, illuminating the leather harnesses hanging on the wall. My gaze sweeps over an array of butt plugs with attached horse tails, and I whimper.

Jack looms so close that my skin tingles with the lick of his ghostly flames.

"Will it hurt?" I ask.

"Pain is a small price to pay for the greatest of pleasure," he growls. "I guarantee you'll never cum harder."

Arousal surges between my legs. I squeeze my thighs together to stem the trickle of moisture. Jack edged me so mercilessly that I'm desperate for any kind of release.

He draws close, his flames burning brighter. I'm certain he senses my excitement.

"Alright," I murmur. "Train me."

"Good girl." Jack pats my ass, his voice warm with approval. "Now, remove the cloak."

51

I shrug the heavy fabric off my shoulders, letting it slide down to the straw-covered floor. The only thing left of my costume are the boots and leather corset, and I feel completely exposed.

Jack's fiery gaze flickers up and down my naked body, and he makes a happy rumble that tightens my nipples. I try not to question how I've already become accustomed to the workings of his eyeholes.

He strides to the wall of horse riding equipment and reaches for a thin leather harness that's structured like a bra. Tapping the side of his breeches, making the kind of clicking noise that will summon a horse.

My breath quickens, and I hurry to his side. It looks like the scene has already begun.

With the gentlest of touches, Jack attaches the harness, fastens its straps around my back, and adjusts it over my boobs. He weighs one breast in his large hand and sighs. "Full udders, thick teats—ready for breeding."

Preening, I pull back my shoulders and shiver as he pulls on a nipple.

"Are you going to be my stallion?" I ask.

His eye flames narrow. "Only if you're a good pony."

Jack gives my nipple one last tweak before selecting what looks like opera-length leather gloves, except they're without finger holes. On closer inspection, they're more like a pair of sleeves.

"What's that?" I ask as Jack eases one of the sheaths over my arm.

"Armbinder," he replies, sounding sinister. "You didn't think I would allow my breeding mare to use her hands."

Moisture floods my folds at the prospect of that juicy cock breeding like an animal.

Jack pulls my bound arm behind my back and shoves the free one into the leather contraption. My back arches, pushing my chest forward as Jack attaches even more straps that hook over my shoulders like a halter.

He walks around me and rubs the base of his pumpkin as though it's a chin. "What a pretty pony you will make."

"There's more?" I ask with a shiver.

"No pony is complete without her headdress."

Jack selects a bridle that matches the harness, complete with blinkers and a pair of leather ears. He places it over my head and fastens the buckle around the back.

"There," he says, his voice light. "Open wide for your bit."

The bit turns out to be a rubber cylinder that attaches to both sides of my bridle. He places it between my teeth before securing it in place.

Jack moves me to the tack table and bends me over its wooden surface. The pulse behind my clit pounds faster as he kicks my legs apart.

"What a lustful little pony," he says. "So wet and eager to be bred."

I groan around my gag, urging him to fill me with that veiny cock. When Jack runs a thick finger down my slit, my core floods with heat. My breath shallows and I push my hips out toward his crotch. I want it hard and rough and relentless. I want him to fuck me until the magic animating him vanishes.

Jack dips two fingers into my pussy, making me shiver. After getting reamed with his gun and the handle of his ax, I need no preparation. I just need to be fucked. Now.

Something warm lands in the cleft of my ass, filling my nostrils with the familiar scent of pumpkin spice. It's Jack's lubricant—the one he used before buggering me with his pistol.

Rolling onto one side, I glance over my shoulder, needing to twist even further to see him because of the blinkers. Jack holds a metallic butt plug with a long, horse-hair tail. Fuck. Is he going to stick that in my ass?

"Hey," I try to say around the bit, but I can't form words. Instead, I shake my head and grunt.

Jack smears the liquid over my asshole. "Do you want to be a good pony?"

My eyes narrow, and I shoot Jack a sidelong glower. The answer is no if it means prancing about with a long tail swishing behind my back.

"Good little ponies get to cum, and bad ponies get the crop." To emphasize his point, Jack steps back and pulls his fingers out of my pussy.

My gaze darts to an array of canes, horse whips, dressage whips, and riding crops, and I shake my head. I came here for his penis, not punishment.

I flare my nostrils. "Fine," I mumble around the bit. "Give me the fucking tail."

Jack's filthy laugh makes my spine tingle, and the sensation only gets worse when he works the warm lubricant into my asshole. I groan, wanting to tell him that I'm still loose from his pistol, but his fingers feel so good.

Slumping against the table, I shudder as Jack scissors his fingers in and out of my ass. Every so often, his pinky reaches down, rubs my clit, and sends a jolt of sensation down my inner thighs.

"Good girl," he rumbles. "Such a docile little slut."

I groan. "Just stick it in me. I'm ready."

Jack either can't understand my mangled words or chooses to ignore them. He's so focused on stretching out my asshole that his panting breaths fan over my skin like a caress.

"Here it comes," he says in a voice deep enough to shake my bones.

He slides out his fingers, replacing them with the tip of

the buttplug. Cold metal pushes against my asshole, getting wider and wider with each encroaching inch. I pant hard through the rubber bit, my thighs trembling. It's already twice as thick as the pistol.

Jack continues pushing it inside until it feels like he's splitting me open. My pussy clenches and releases, wishing it was the one being filled, while my poor asshole is gaping.

What kind of sorcery is this? The plug didn't look so big, earlier.

"Relax, little pony." Jack rubs circles on my asscheek. "The view from where I am standing is incredible."

Strangely, I find his praise comforting, easing all the tightness in my sphincter muscles. The rest of the plug enters my ass with a pleasant slide.

I'm feeling satisfyingly full and ready to be pounded into the table.

Jack gives my ass a gentle squeeze. "Pretty pony, see how the horsehairs rub your hungry cunt?"

He steps back, letting the tail fall between my spread cheeks. As the rough hairs sweep down to my pussy and graze my clit, I straighten. When am I going to get fucked?

Turning around, I drop my gaze to Jack's breeches, which strain with the largest, most obscene-looking erection. Saliva floods my mouth. I slip my tongue over the rubber gag, desperate for another taste.

As if reading my mind, he says, "You may bite and suck on the bit to your heart's content."

"I'd rather suck your cock," I mumble around the bit with a moan.

A plume of flames curls from Jack's pumpkin maw. I think that's his way of grinning. Without another word, he attaches a pair of reins to the bridle, turns on his heel, and heads toward the stall's exit.

My eyes widen. "I thought we were going to have sex?"

The reins pull my bridle as he strides out into the stable's walkway. I stumble after him at a forward angle, as I can't even splay my arms out for balance.

"Careful now," Jack says without turning around.

I glare at the back of his pumpkin. That's easy for him to say. He's not the one trussed up like a horny show pony.

"Where are we going?" I mumble around the bit.

"To the breeding shed. There's only so much beauty a man can stand before can't resist his pony's sweet cunt."

Chapter Eight

Trotting after Jack, I pass the stall housing his demonic horse. I'm so excited at the prospect of getting sex, that I forget to cringe away from the creature's fiery glare. I don't even flinch when it neighs a plume of smoke from a maw filled with sharp teeth.

Snatching my gaze from the other equine, I follow Jack out into a courtyard illuminated by oil lamps, and it feels like I've stepped into another century. My boots even clip-clop over the cobblestones.

Jack gives my reins a gentle tug and leads me across the yard to a mausoleum on the edge of Whitechapel Cemetery. It's twice the size of a garden shed but made of stone. Above the four pillars holding up its pediment are an engraving of the words, NEMO MALUS FELIX.

I'm pretty sure it means 'no rest for the wicked.'

My throat tightens, and my steps falter. There's no logical reason why I'm getting the jitters. Jack's already a malevolent spirit, and he's been good to me so far... Apart from all that pussy teasing.

He pauses at the doorway. "Scared, Beautiful Bess?"

I give my head a vigorous shake. It's not like I can form coherent sentences.

"Good girl." With a wave of his hand, he opens the door.

Moonlight illuminates its stone walls. The interior is empty, save for a stone coffin engraved with:

JOHN RANN
31 OCTOBER 1750 to
30 NOVEMBER 1774
NEMO MALUS FELIX

Before I can ponder why there's the same Latin phrase both here and on the mausoleum's exterior, Jack places a large hand between my shoulder blades and bends me on the coffin's cool, stone surface.

Shivers skitter across my skin. This isn't right. We shouldn't be desecrating someone's grave. I turn my head, trying to voice my concern, but he grabs a handful of my hair and twists it around the reins.

"If you're worried about getting fucked over someone's dead body, don't," he says, his voice rough. "This coffin belongs to me."

The tension in my shoulders eases, and I relax onto the stone. Somehow, knowing that Jack's corpse remains are inside is reassuring.

He runs his hand over my ass, his breath fanning across my skin. It's hard, hurried, and hungry. When his clothed erection presses against my pussy, it feels like I'm about to be devoured.

"Can you handle a cock of my size, sweet slut?" he croons. "Can you take it fast and rough? Because when I start, I won't stop, even if it hurts."

I give him a vigorous nod and try to push back against his hardness.

He twists the buttplug, sending sparks of pleasure across my nerves. I gasp, my knees hitting the wall of the coffin.

Jack parts my outer lips with his fingers and runs the tip of his bare cock up and down my slit, making the most obscene wet noises. "You are dripping, pretty pony. Is all of that for me?"

Nodding, I mewl around my gag, my hips tilting, my thighs parting. He's teased me to the point of insanity, and I need him right now.

Jack pushes into my pussy with an excruciating slowness that prolongs the most delicious stretch. He's about two inches inside—barely enough to sheathe his tip when he pulls out.

I push back with an urgent need, but Jack holds me in place against the stone.

"Good ponies stay still when they're breeding if they want to cum," he rasps into my ear.

Fuck.

He doesn't even give me the chance to nod before he enters me again with a sharp thrust.

It's both pain and pleasure and a powerful stretch. My mouth opens in a mangled scream. He's even bigger than I thought, even thicker, and his cock settles so deeply inside me that I can barely breathe.

My organs shift, and my muscles spasm around his girth. I've never in my life felt this full, and the butt plug makes things a hundred times more intense.

Jack's cock is the sweetest agony. My skin feels like it's been set alight with the flames of rapture, and ecstasy burns along my nerves. I'm being fucked by a dead man, but I have never felt so alive.

He pulls back, leaving me needy. I whimper, already impatient for another thrust. One shuddering breath later, he snaps his hips, entering me again and again at a brutal pace.

My thighs tremble with the onslaught, and I moan around my bit. Sex with Jack is incredible.

I seldom climax with William in doggy style unless I'm rubbing my clit, but each of Jack's long, deep strokes hits that special spot inside me with perfect accuracy. I tremble so much that the only thing keeping me from shattering on the floor is the stone coffin.

"You make such pretty noises, Bess," he says with a deep thrust that makes me choke. "But I think you can do better."

"Wait," I mumble around the bit. "What do you mean—"

Jack picks up the pace, pounding into me harder and faster than is humanly possible. I cry out around the gag, my heart thundering. It's like being attached to a fuck machine powered by lightning.

"Just like that," he says, his voice breathy. "You are taking my cock so well."

I'm shaking, hyperventilating, and blinking back tears. This is more than I can handle. "J-Jack!"

I thrash from side to side, but it's impossible with my arms in a leather binder and his weight on my back. He shows no mercy and fucks me hard and deep. It's heaven. It's hell. It's every wicked pleasure in between.

"You're going to cum around my dick," he growls. "I want you screaming loud enough to wake the dead."

Jack shifts position a fraction and hammers my g-spot.

My vision explodes with stars.

For a moment, it feels like I really am a pony, galloping through the night, over turbulent waters. Wave after wave of sensation crashes over my senses, immersing me in a sea of bliss.

Jack pulls on my reins, guiding me through the current, his presence the only thing keeping me from drowning. Cumming with Jack at the reins gives new meaning to the phrase la petite mort.

Spasms seize my pussy and travel down my every limb. The orgasm engulfs my entire body—I'm lost in this insane climax.

For the briefest of moments, I see specters. They dance and float on the edges of my vision, which is impossible because I'm wearing blinkers. Throughout this, Jack slows his thrusts and rides out the waves of my climax, making it last.

His chest vibrates with a satisfied growl. "You squeeze my shaft tighter than any fist. What a very good girl."

I clench even harder around his cock, which swells impossibly wider.

Jack shudders and moans with what feels to be a powerful orgasm. Once again, it's a dry climax, but I'm still too tingly to consider why.

The erection inside me pulses again and again until Jack slumps against my back, breathing hard as he slows his thrusts.

"I have waited centuries for a girl like you," he murmurs so quietly that I can almost dismiss what I'm hearing as my own wishful thinking.

My eyelids grow heavy, and I melt into the stone, my mind drifting to a peculiar thought.

Isn't it strange that I would have the best sex of my life with a man almost as unavailable as William? Jack might be an ax-murdering ghost who only appears one night a year, but at least he's been honest.

I still can't understand why William bought me that diamond ring if he wanted to farm me out to his uncles.

Actually, I do.

The only way to secure my help with running the firm is to keep me subservient and degraded. He wanted me easy to control. He had to understand that all the years I spent working for his father made me indispensable.

I wait for the hurt, the betrayal, the anguish, but Jack's cock makes a pleasant twitch, and I'm too steeped in the afterglow to care. Jack hasn't just given me the best sex of my life. The gold he's promised will protect me from William's revenge.

As he pulls out, I plant my feet back on the floor and raise my upper body. Shivering and panting, I ready myself to stand.

That was incredible.

What a pity living men can't fuck so thoroughly or so well.

As I raise my chest, Jack winds his hand around my hair again, and he pushes me back down on the coffin. "I'm not finished with you yet, Wench."

"What?" I mumble around the gag.

He shoves back into me with a thrust hard enough to make me see double. "We have all night, remember? I wager I'll be fucking you until the crack of dawn."

Chapter Nine

J ack fucks me for hours on that stone coffin at a punishing pace. It's as though he's making up for two and a half centuries of abstinence.

I briefly wonder if he ever encountered another woman on the road, and something in my chest burns hotter than Jack's flames. Why am I catching feelings over what can only be a one-night stand?

Another orgasm drags me into unconsciousness, and I finally understand why he took so long to start fucking. Dead men, especially those powered by magic, don't need to rest between erections.

When I resurface, I'm free of my restraints and nestled in his strong arms. I'm not sure how much time has passed —it could be minutes or hours or half the night, but only a ghost of sensation remains from the butt plug.

My pussy, however, twinges.

I open my eyes to find Jack carrying me through a doorway and into another stone chamber.

"What is this place?" I rasp.

"You didn't think I would let you rest atop a coffin?" he asks with a chuckle.

Actually, I kind of did.

This room is palatial compared to what I first saw of the crypt. Flames dance within iron wall sconces, bathing the space in yellow light. We pass a stone frieze that says, NEMO MALUS FELIX.

Jack stops at a bed made of four stone posts adorned with curtains as thin as spider webs. My gaze lands on the words inscribed on the canopy rail.

"Nemo malus Felix?" I ask. "That's the fourth time I've seen that phrase."

"It's a curse that means no peace for the wicked," he replies, his voice laced with bitterness. "My eternal punishment for robbing a chaplain."

I frown as he lays me on a mattress as soft and as springy as moss and wait for him to explain the details of this curse. When Jack doesn't elaborate, I raise myself on my elbows.

He sits beside me on the mattress, not making it dip, and massages the tension out of my shoulders. It doesn't work because I have questions. Questions about the curse. Questions about why he kills. Questions about what he does all year when it's not Halloween.

"You were executed, right?" I ask.

"Aye," he growls.

"But even that's an unfair punishment for highway robbery. Why would you also get cursed?"

He stares at me through those flaming eyes. Eyes that burn with the fires of hell. A knot tightens in my stomach. Did I ask too much?

The flames dim, and he sighs. "You would have sympathy for a sinner?"

My brows rise. What a peculiar thing to ask. "These days England doesn't execute people for robbery—not even murder. Did you kill anyone when you were a highwayman?"

"No." He pauses for longer than the moment warrants before adding, "Not while I was alive. Since my death, hundreds have lost their heads under my blade."

I bite down on my bottom lip. It's strange how a man can fuck a woman senseless to the point she forgets he's an ax-murdering ghoul.

"What happens to them?" I ask.

"Some of their spirits go to heaven." He hesitates. "Others, I meet in hell."

My jaw drops. "Wait. Did you say—"

"Hush, Beautiful Bess," he murmurs. "Do not spoil my last hour of heaven."

My jaw clicks shut. No one has ever described having sex with me as anything, let alone heavenly. I drop my gaze from his pumpkin to the shadows dancing along the net curtains. Even if Jack doesn't seem distraught, it's still unjust that he's subject to something so vindictive.

I thought my situation with William was bad but Jack's is a thousand times worse. The part of me that's grateful for tonight's pleasure wants to help, but I can't think how. The best thing I can do right now is to keep him distracted until the end of the night. I have all year to research ways to break his curse or save his soul.

Sliding down the bed, Jack wraps an arm around my shoulders and pulls me into his chest. He runs a hand up and down my back, the soft caresses making my eyelids flutter closed.

"Tonight has been wonderful," I say with a sigh. "I've never been so thoroughly satisfied."

Jack draws back to stare down at me, his flames blazing. "Surely you have a devoted lover."

69

"Not so devoted," I mutter. "I broke off the engagement after he told me to suck his uncles' cocks."

"Why would he do that?"

I don't want to waste Jack's last hours explaining how much William needs me to run the family business. Or how he's so desperate to impress his uncles that he tried to reframe me as a no-limits slut. So, I give him the simple version.

"His uncles weren't impressed with his choice of fiancée, so he wanted me to demonstrate my skills."

Jack growls. "A bastard like that belongs in hell. He should be your protector, not your panderer. You are a beauty capable of attracting an endless amount of willing suitors."

"Are you kidding?" I huff a laugh. "Men like William don't appreciate women unless they're tall, blonde, and thin."

He cups the side of my face with his large, leathery hand. "In my day, men would kill for your attention. Painters would sell their souls to capture a face and body as comely as yours."

William once described my figure as Rubenesque, which I didn't take as a compliment, but hearing those words from Jack puts them into a different light.

"Really?" I ask, hungry to hear more.

He threads his fingers through my curls. "The last time I saw hair as pretty as this was on a portrait of Queen Elizabeth." Then he runs the pad of his thumb over my cheekbone and then my mouth. "You have eyes bluer than cornflowers on a summer's day and lips the color of poppies."

My heart flutters. Jack certainly has a way with words.

"You're a natural beauty, Bess. No one can tell me any different."

My breath catches. He's been calling me that the entire night, but it didn't register until now. No one has ever called me beautiful—not without an ulterior motive. No one ever elaborated, either.

Jack's fingers slide down my neck, breaking my skin out in pleasant shivers. He lingers over my collarbones before cupping my breast. "Big, beautiful tits and thick nipples I would kill to suck."

I arch into his touch.

Jack slides his hand down to my waist and over my hips. "The kind of curved waist and round belly I've only seen on sculptures of goddesses. And the rest..."

He groans, his fingers clutching my thighs.

Every inch of my body trembles, and I can't get enough of his words. "What about it?"

"I wish I could taste your skin," he rumbles. "Wish I could feast on your cunt. But most of all, I wish I could kiss your sweet lips."

My chest tightens. He can't do much with that pumpkin.

"What happened to your head?" I ask. "Surely it would have accompanied you in death."

"I wasn't beheaded."

The flames in his eye holes dim, and he sucks in a huge breath. It's almost like he's closing his eyes.

"Jack?"

"After I was hanged, no priest would bless my soul, so my spirit hovered beside my swinging corpse." He pauses. "Later, the executioner cut me down and threw my carcass into a shallow grave, but two nights later, I was dug up by body snatchers."

My pulse quickens, and I grab Jack's lapels. "Why?"

"They dragged it into the stables. I could do nothing but follow."

"What happened next?" I whisper.

"They handed me over to the chaplain I robbed," he snarls. "That sanctimonious bastard crowed over my corpse. He boasted about sending a hedge witch to seduce me and perform spells while I slept. He said this plan was a year in the making."

"No."

"Then he hacked off my head with an ax and began a ritual that condemned me to cleanse the street of highway robbers."

My jaw drops. "But why would he go so far?"

"Revenge for stealing gold entrusted to him by Princess Amelia," he says, his voice bitter. "It wasn't enough for me to die. He wanted me miserable in recompense for losing favor in the royal court."

"But that's not fair." I shake my head. "Is that why you chop off people's heads?"

All the air leaves him in an instant, and he slumps back on the mattress. "He compelled me to be a killer. Compelled me to purge the streets of highwaymen and their descendants. Compelled me to watch myself rob the innocent of their lives."

Tears sting the backs of my eyes. How could someone be so vengeful? Jack died for his crimes, but the bastard who cursed him still wasn't satisfied. Jack must have targeted me because one of my ancestors had been a highwayman. It explains why the police never noticed a pile of corpses every year. Jack's profile of victims is extremely narrow.

But there's something else I need to ask.

"Why did you show me mercy?"

Flames curl from his mouth. "Would you believe that my desire for you was greater than the compulsion to kill?"

I suck in a sharp breath and lean back into the mattress, my gaze unfocusing. Nobody ever chose me over anything.

Especially not William. That bastard only wanted me to help him run the family firm. The thought that I could distract Jack from a powerful curse is perplexing, but it has to be true.

"Wow…" I shake off my stupor. "A-are you sure?"

Jack turns onto his side, looking me full in the face. The intensity of his flames makes my heart flip.

"You have no idea how happy I am that we crossed paths," he murmurs. "And not just because you saved me from murdering. I am drawn to the purity of your soul. It has been an eternity since I have encountered a woman as beautiful as she is bawdy. In all my years, no matter when I was alive and handsome, I have never felt such satisfaction."

"What do you mean?" I whisper.

"You enjoyed everything I gave you tonight." He presses closer, his clothed cock grinding against my pussy. "No matter how depraved. You didn't condemn me for my perversions—you climaxed."

Heat rises to my cheeks, and I lower my lashes. "I enjoyed being bred like a pony, but to be honest, it was all about your cock."

His deep growl sends tingles across my skin, and sensation rushes to my aching pussy. How on earth could I want more sex after being so thoroughly fucked?

"Look at me, Beautiful Bess," Jack rasps.

I drag my gaze up his buttoned jacket, over his cravat and the curve of his pumpkin, and meet flames that burn so bright they could incinerate my soul.

"Dawn approaches. Will you give me one last moment of joy?"

My pussy clenches. Jack doesn't even need to ask.

"How do you want it?"

He leans flat on his back. "Ride me," he rumbles. "Ride me like a stallion until the curse drags me back to hell."

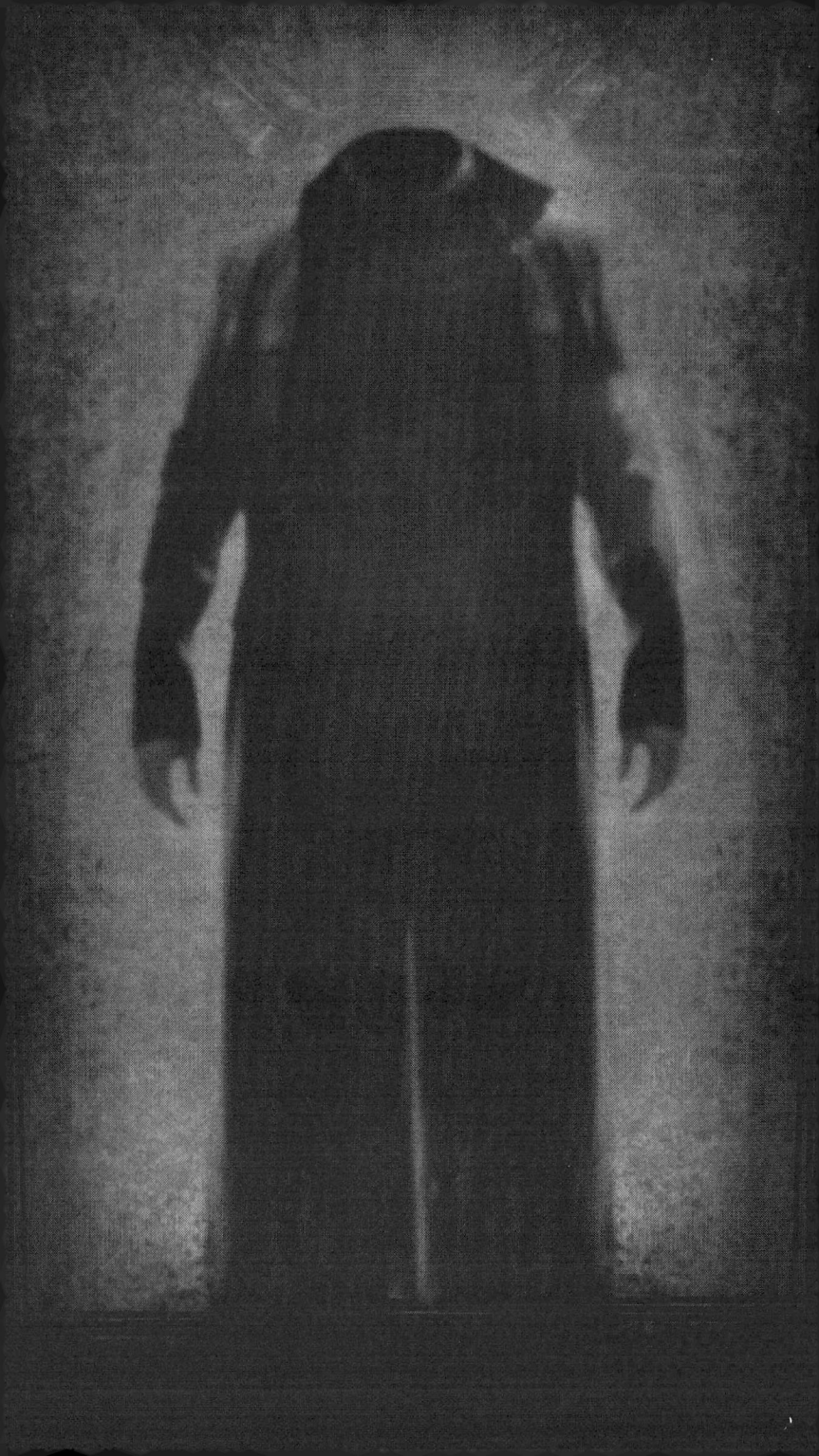

Chapter Ten

My gaze darts to the erection straining through Jack's breeches, and my pussy floods with heat. I want to ride that fat cock until our time ends, but I can't.

Something Jack said is troubling.

"You just said you're going to hell after this," I rasp. "But I thought you lived here—"

"Bess." Jack sits up, his hand cupping the side of my neck.

There's nothing threatening about the touch—it's almost tender—but it stops the surge of questions.

"This crypt was my dwelling for the first few decades after I died when the curse drove me to purge the roads of highwaymen and other cutthroats. And when dawn broke on the morn of All Saints Day, my spirit returned here to fester."

My breaths turn shallow, barely grazing the tops of my lungs. I should interrupt him, take out his cock, and distract him from finishing the rest of his story. There's no point since my mind has already raced ahead and filled in the gaps.

"Eventually, most rogues knew not to travel these roads on October thirty-first," Jack says, his voice pained, "When I could find no sinners, the curse drove me to kill their descendants."

"Innocents."

Jack grunts. "Innocents."

"That's when you first went to hell?"

"Aye. The first rays of the sun burned like hellfire," he croaks. "Then the next thing I knew, I was dragged into the seventh circle of hell."

A lump forms in my throat as I catch the reference. So, Dante's inferno is real. My memory of The Divine Comedy is sketchy, but I'm sure that's where they tortured the souls of sinners into a river of boiling blood.

"What was it like?" Words tumble from my lips before I can stop them.

Fuck, I'm being so intrusive.

"Bess." The flames in his eye holes dim as though I've dampened his mood. "I do not wish to spend my last hour in the living world dwelling on impending torment."

"Sorry." I place a hand over his chest, my fingers sinking into the silk of his jacket.

Jack seems a little less solid than before, but I don't have the heart to ask why. It's probably due to his curse. He's like a murderous Cinderella, waiting for the sun to rise instead of the clock to strike midnight.

"What made you start robbing people in the first place?" I ask, trying to change the subject.

"Life was shit when I was alive," he rumbles. "Anyone not born into riches was guaranteed a life of drudgery until they suffered a pauper's death.

"Did you have parents?"

He grunts. "My mother was a maid, and I never knew my father. She died when I was young, and all I had was my uncle, a coachman who taught me how to tend to horses."

I lean against him and sigh. "How did you go from that to robbery?"

"Stupidity. Greed. Frustration," he says. "I wanted to be more than just a servant. The feeling only got worse when my uncle got trampled by a horse, and there was no money to pay for a surgeon."

My breath hitches. "What happened to him?"

"He lost his job and moved into my living quarters. I did what I could to help, but he suffered a slow and painful death.

"That's awful."

"That's life," he replies. "I learned that the only way to thrive in that world was to take what I needed to survive."

I imagine him stealing his employer's horse and holding up stagecoaches with his pistols. "That's when you became a highwayman?"

He chuckles. "I started picking pockets to pay for my uncle's upkeep. He died when I was fourteen. By then, I was already used to the easy money."

Jack's voice flattens when he describes spending years stealing to pay off his uncle's debts and funeral expenses until he saved enough money to purchase a horse.

Closing my eyes, I wonder how different my life would have gone had I been born in a century without foster care. If I'm honest with myself, William's behavior wasn't a complete shock. I dismissed his red flags, telling myself he was just open-minded about sex.

In hindsight, I see that William was preparing me all along for that encounter with his uncles. I thought I was dating up when I was really dating down.

"Robbing coaches paid off my debts, gave me a home, status, security," he says.

"I get it."

He huffs a bitter laugh. "Ten years of living well in exchange for centuries of torment. If I had my time again, I would choose to die as a pauper."

An ache forms in my chest. "Gosh, Jack... I'm so sorry."

He wraps his fingers around my wrist. "I regret many things. If I had chosen honest employment. I would never have robbed a man so bent on vengeance. Perhaps my soul would now be at rest."

My breath hitches and the backs of my eyes burn. I want to tell Jack that I will help break his curse, but I can't give him false hope. All I can do is research.

"Only one thing has made the centuries of torment worthwhile," he rumbles.

"What?"

His fingers slide down my hand to intertwine with mine. "Meeting you."

A surge of emotion has my eyes snapping open. No one, not even William has ever expressed such deep appreciation. My fiancé's proposal was a four-word affair with a five-carat diamond but it came with the worst kind of strings. Strings like sharing me with other men.

Jack is the complete opposite. He'd galloped away the moment sirens approached, saying he didn't want intruders to look at what was his for the night.

Me.

"Will you send me to heaven with your cunt, my beautiful Bess?" he asks.

"Any time," I reply, my voice choked. "You never need to ask."

Jack releases my hand, letting me slip my fingers over his muscular thigh into the placket of his breeches. The rest of his body might not be as solid as before, but his cock is harder than iron. As I ease it out, he makes a sizzling hiss.

The erection in my hand pulses, feeling more vibrant than real life. It's almost as though he's channeling all sensation, all magic, into that fat cock.

Jack shivers, his breath quickening. "Bess," he says in a voice so commanding that I rise off the bed. "Don't make me wait."

His muscular thighs harden as I straddle his hips. I try not to think about what it's costing him to maintain his physical form, so I focus on giving him a sexy memory to cherish while he's in hell.

Gripping the base of Jack's shaft with one hand, I hover over his erection.

Jack takes my other hand, holding me steady as I rub his bulbous tip against my wet slit. The magic must be concentrated there or maybe some of his flames because a burst of ecstasy sears my clit.

"Fuck," he says with a moan. "You know how to tease a man. Please, I beg, sheathe me into that tight, wet cunt."

Positioning him to my opening, I lower my hips and sink down on his glorious, thick shaft. The stretch is so pleasurable it borders on pain. He's splitting me wide open, burning me from the inside until every nerve crackles with molten heat.

"Oh my god," I say with a gasp.

"I appreciate the sentiment," he growls, "But you should call me Jack."

My teeth clamp down on my bottom lip. "F-Fuck."

Most men would become impatient with my slow pace and buck their hips, but Jack lies beneath me, his fingers closing in around mine. He's so big, so thick, so solid... It's still hard to believe I'm fucking a ghost.

I slide down his length, inch by delicious inch, my skin breaking out in a sweat. Moonlight shining in through the thin drapes fades, leaving the only source of light coming from within his pumpkin.

Jack's chest rumbles, reminding me of a feline's purr. I'm gasping, shuddering, twitching around his girth. This new angle is more intense than the one before and places delicious weight on my g-spot.

"So tight," he says, his voice strangled.

My pussy spasms, desperately trying to adjust. I ask, "Should I move?"

"No." He grabs my hips.

"What's wrong?".

"Stay there for a minute," he rumbles. "I want to commit your beauty to memory. I need this moment to last."

"A-alright."

"Look at me," he says in a voice that seems so far away.

My breath hitches. Until now, I haven't truly looked Jack in the eye. My gaze mostly focuses on the pumpkin's orange exterior, the jagged mouth, and even the flames. But the eyes are the windows to the soul.

If I stare directly into those triangular holes, will I see the magic or the outer circles of hell? Or would I find Jack's condemned spirit?

My gaze sweeps toward Jack's eye holes. The flames burn less brightly, but there's enough light for me to take in the imperfections on the pumpkin's orange skin. Deep grooves run vertically making it look smaller than before, along with patches of white. I'm not entirely sure what this means.

"Please," he rasps.

With a deep breath, I stare into the flames.

"Bess," he says, his voice breathy. "I can see your soul."

"What?"

He clasps my hands. "Forgive me."

"Why?"

"I have spent so long seeing nothing but demons and despair and the denizens of hell. I wanted to gaze upon something pure."

I'm nowhere close to being innocent. Not after reading so much smut. Not after reenacting so many of my favorite sex scenes with William. Especially not after what I've done tonight with Jack.

My lips tighten. William didn't think I was pure. That wretched bastard assumed I would jump on his uncles' withered cocks, just because he asked. All this time, he assumed I was some kind of no-limits slut he could farm out to other men.

My attention drifts back to Jack.

"But isn't there a circle of hell for the lustful?"

He huffs. "There is no sin in the enjoyment of sex. The second circle punishes those who twist those desires to the detriment of others."

Like my ex fiancé, who tried to coerce me into sucking off his uncles? I swallow hard and remind myself why Jack wanted to lock gazes.

"M-my soul is really pure?"

"I see your kindness, your giving heart, your self-respect. I even see your pain. You are even more lovely on the inside."

A weight lifts from my heart, and the muscles of my pussy relax. Jack's words are a balm on the blisters from my encounter with William and his uncles. And Jack is also right. People should be able to enjoy sex without being shamed or condemned. My clit pulses, desperate for some friction.

Holding onto Jack's gloved hands, I raise my hips, placing my weight on my knees. Jack's cockhead rubs against my g spot.

"Oh."

"Good girl," Jack rumbles. "Just like that. Take what you need to satisfy that needy cunt."

I lower myself down again, shuddering as he grazes that sensitive patch. Up and down, up and down, I chase my pleasure, building up a steady rhythm that makes Jack groan.

"You should see the view from down here," he says. "You should see the way your tits bounce."

One of his hands releases mine to play with my nipple. The rolling of his gloved fingers sends bolts of electricity to my core.

"Come closer. I want those huge tits rubbing on my chest."

I lean forward letting my nipples brush against the silk of his frock coat. This new position provides a delicious sensation against my clit, sending a pulse of pleasure that tightens my pussy.

"So greedy," Jack groans, his arms wrapping around my back, pulling my chest flush against his. "So mine."

The up-and-down movements become more difficult in this position, so I circle my hips. My clit rubs over the wads of silk, creating delicious tension and the faint beginnings of an orgasm.

Jack's hands slide down my back, so he's cupping my ass and guiding my movements. Each gentle thrust fills my core with sparks, and I cling to his shoulders.

I'm staring so deeply into those triangular eye slits that I see a face in the flames. The visage gazing back at me has arched brows, angular cheekbones, and a strong jaw. It's not a monster or a murderer but a man.

"Jack," I whisper. "Is that you?"

"You see me?" He raises his upper body, resting his weight on his arms.

Arousal gathers as I slide further down that thick cock, making me gasp.

"Um... I think so."

Jack's pumpkin is so close to my face that the flames within it heat my lips. I press a kiss on its warm surface.

"Do that again" he groans.

Placing both hands on the side of the gourd, I pepper its surface with kisses, all the while riding Jack's cock like hellhounds are snapping at our heels. They are because we're running out of time.

"I wish I really could send you to heaven," I murmur.

Jack groans, this time sounding bittersweet. He thrusts his hips, fucking me as deep and as hard as I'm fucking him. "The time I've spent with you is a slice of paradise I will cherish forever."

"You'll remember me?" I ask through panting breaths, meeting him thrust for thrust.

"Fuck," he grinds out. "I can't hold on much longer. How could I forget the woman who fulfilled my every fantasy?"

I ride him harder, faster like he really is my stallion. There's friction against my nipples, my g spot, my cervix, and my clit. The only thing stopping me from self-combusting is the magic.

Bright light streams in through the gossamer drapes. I concentrate on the man staring at me through the flames. If we don't acknowledge it, maybe dawn will never arrive.

The build-up is no longer gradual. My orgasm gallops closer, accelerating to the beat of my heart. I shove back the sensations and grit my teeth. If I cum, the night will end. If I cum, he'll disappear without knowing what's in my heart.

"J-Jack—"

"Yes?" he replies.

"Could I meet you here next year?"

SIGGY SHADE

"You would see me again?" His voice is breathy with awe. "But I'll have no sovereigns to offer once I've given you my stash."

"I don't want—" Before I can complete my sentence, sensation tears through me in a powerful orgasm.

The pleasure is overwhelming. I feel it in my pussy, my gut, my chest. Pure ecstasy takes over and pushes out a scream. I cling to Jack, my hips still riding, my pussy squeezing and pulsing around his girth.

Jack jerks back with a roar. Powerful pulses seize his cock, pushing my climax deeper.

I can't breathe for several moments. I can't even speak, but it takes an effort to fight through the sensations to force out the words, "I don't want the gold. I want you."

He stills. "Bess?"

The pumpkin falls off his head and rolls to the end of the mattress. I lurch to the side, trying to catch it but I over-balance and miss.

Jack's head drops down to the stone floor with a sickening thud.

84

Chapter Eleven

I draw in a sharp breath through my teeth and scramble to the edge of the bed.

Jack's pumpkin lies smashed into four pieces on a stone floor littered with pulp and seeds.

My stomach lurches. What on earth does this mean?

"Bess." His voice is a whisper in the breeze.

I turn back to the mattress to find myself sitting on a pile of clothes.

"Jack?"

I grab the glove. It's as light as leather. I fumble at the neck of his jacket, but there's no sight of Jack.

He's gone.

Gone back to hell.

Back to a punishment he didn't deserve.

I sit back on my heels and moan. "But we didn't even get to say goodbye."

Streams of bright light hit the side of my face. It's far too dazzling to be the morning sun. Peering through a thick curtain of spiderwebs, I stare at the crumbling walls to find approaching headlights.

"What?"

I turn back to what's left of Jack. His clothes have gone and what I thought was a mattress is a stone altar overrun with moss.

"Shit!"

I launch myself off the platform, landing on an uneven and crumbling floor. Cold wind blows in through the broken stonework, chilling my skin. This isn't a mausoleum —it's a ruin.

And there's no sign of the broken pumpkin.

My stomach lurches, and I clutch at my chest. How much of tonight was real?

Everything aches—my nipples, my asshole, my pussy. I've never been fucked so hard or so thoroughly. But none of this makes sense.

Headlights drench the interior with light, and I wrap an arm around my bare breasts and place a hand over my naked crotch. What the hell am I going to do?

Car doors open and close.

Shit.

Nobody can find me here, dressed only in a leather corset and boots.

If I'm lucky, they'll think I'm crazy.

If I'm not...

A shudder runs down my spine.

I need to hide.

Stepping back into the ruin's darkest corner, I stumble over something that splinters underfoot. It's a chest, half-buried in the floor. Its wooden top is shattered, revealing a stash of gold coins.

An ache forms in my chest, and my eyes sting with tears. Jack wasn't my imagination—he was real.

"I don't want your sovereigns," I whisper. "I want you, Jack."

Footsteps approach like thunder.

I sprint toward the corner and try to meld into the rough stonework.

"In here, Sarge," says a male voice.

Someone floods the chamber with a beam so bright I have to squint.

Fuck.

Two huge police officers step in through the doorway, blocking the only exit. They stare down at me like I've escaped an asylum.

"Elizabeth Bryan?" one of them asks.

I cringe.

There's only one reason they know my name.

William must have sent them after me for taking the car.

His partner steps forward, his palms raised. He's about the same age as William's uncles with a toothbrush mustache. From the flat cap he wears, I'm guessing he's the sergeant.

The sergeant's gaze rakes down my body. "Are you Elizabeth Bryan, former employee of Whitechapel Finance?"

"Of course, she is," says a voice that sets my teeth on edge. "She's still wearing the tracker."

My hand twitches toward my hair. That bastard must have slipped something into my braid when he grabbed me in the courtyard.

William stumbles in, still wearing his highwayman's cloak and mask. He pushes past the officers and gapes.

"Why are you only wearing a corset and boots?" He folds his arms across his chest and sneers. "Is this an attempt to slither out of your predicament? It won't work."

I scowl and raise my chin. William might have caught me with my pants down, but he's crazy if he thinks he can shame me into cowering.

Since the flashlights are pointed at where I'm crouching,

nobody notices the half-buried sovereigns. I make an effort not to look its way. If I'm ever going to find a means to save Jack's soul, I'll need every ounce of that gold.

"You're in a lot of trouble," William says, his voice giddy with glee. "Theft and vandalism of a company vehicle. Theft of a five-carat family heirloom."

"That ring belongs to me," I snap.

He stalks toward me, his features hardening. "Uncle Thomas will make sure you waste what's left of your twenties in prison."

My throat tightens. William loves having me at his mercy. I can't believe I didn't notice the glaring red flags until tonight.

"Do you want to press charges, Mr. Whitechapel?" asks the sergeant.

William narrows his eyes. "I could be persuaded to drop the charges if she apologizes nicely to the family."

He wants me to go back to the manor with him and finish what he tried to start with those perverts. Fuck him. I've survived an ax-wielding specter cursed to take my head. I'll survive his revenge.

I turn to the two policemen, my lip curling. "My ex-fiancé wants me to have sex with his uncles. That's the reason why I left."

They stare down at me as though I haven't just accused William of sexual coercion. Either they don't believe my side of the story or they don't give a shit. From the donations Whitechapel Finance makes to the Police Charitable Trust, I can safely assume it's the latter.

"Your answer?" William snarls.

"I'm still an employee of Whitechapel Finance." I turn back to the officers, my breath quickening. "William didn't put my dismissal in writing. Even if he did, I'm still entitled to a notice period. Don't let him rope you into a scandal."

He shakes his head. "She can't even apologize and make amends. Put her under arrest."

The sergeant advances.

My heart pounds loud enough to wake the dead.

"No." I try to step back, but there's nowhere to go.

"Come quietly, Madam, or we'll use force." The sergeant reaches for one of my arms.

I hiss a breath through my teeth.

Fuck. So much for my courage.

I'm freezing, half naked, and defenseless. No matter what I do next, I'm screwed.

Lowering into a deeper crouch, I hiss, "Don't touch me!"

"You have my permission to use force," William drawls.

The constable hands the flashlight to his superior and wrenches me up by the arm, exposing my breasts. I kick and scream, but he twists my arm behind my back.

He presses his erection into my ass, leans into me, and growls, "You are resisting arrest."

"Let go of me!" I scream.

William nudges the leering sergeant. "She's not much to look at but she has a skilled mouth."

"Fuck you." I throw my body back against the constable and kick William with both legs.

He doubles over with a roar. "Bitch. Now, you've made matters worse."

I clench my jaw. The next one who so much as looks at me funny will get a kick in the teeth.

A loud bang has us all jumping. The constable releases my arms before stumbling to the floor.

"What was that?" The sergeant lowers the flashlight and reaches for the radio on his chest. Before he can even call for help, there's another loud bang, and he falls to his knees.

Stomach lurching, I whirl around, expecting to find

someone standing by the altar. The flintlock pistols float from behind the curtain of spiderwebs.

My pulse races. I glance around for their owner, but that side of the ruin is empty.

"Jack?" I whisper, my voice trembling. "Is that you?"

"Who's Jack?" William grabs my arm and spins me around. He barely casts the fallen officers a glance before snarling, "Is that why you're naked? You've been fucking someone else?"

"Let go." I shove him in the chest.

William stumbles back a step but pulls me into his chest like a shield. He wraps his fingers around my throat and roars, "Jack or whoever the fuck you are. Drop the guns, or I'll crush the whore's throat."

I grind my teeth and kick William in the shin, making him grunt.

Jack can't be here—the magic already sent him to hell. But who operated the pistols?

Thunder rumbles loud enough to shake me to the marrow. William grabs my throat and squeezes. The entire evening flitters through my mind like a kaleidoscope. William reminding me that Sixteen String Jack haunting the roads, the chase down a country road, mind-blowing sex, and Jack telling me that sunrise ended his time in the living world.

My gaze darts to the light still streaming through the walls.

They came from the police car—not the sun.

"Jack?" I rasp.

"Bess." Jack's voice makes the air tremble. "Would you really choose me over the gold?"

"Of course," I say.

William pivots to the side, trying to find Jack. "Show yourself!"

"With pleasure," Jack replies.

He appears before us, huge, solid, clad in his long, black cloak and wielding the double-headed ax. The pumpkin is gone, leaving him headless.

William screams. I take advantage of his shock to elbow him in the ribs, forcing him to release my throat.

As I jump aside, Jack swings his ax overhead and slices through William's neck.

Chapter Twelve

∞∞

I stiffen, unable to take a breath. Even the air is as still as death.

Somehow, the ax left William's body intact and still with his head. He stands for a heartbeat before crumpling to the floor like a broken marionette.

Relief escapes my body in an outward breath, and I place a trembling hand over my chest. The criminal charges, the petty vendetta, the attempt to pass me around to other men—it's over.

The blade of Jack's ax hits the floor with a clang, breaking me from my thoughts.

Jack's broad chest rises and falls with noisy breaths, but I can't stop staring at the empty space over his collar. He's returned headless and without the pumpkin. What on earth can that mean?

"He is your fiancé," Jack says, his voice flat.

My brows pull together. Is he jealous? "I broke up with William minutes before you rode after my car, remember? He's been hunting me since and even brought the police."

Jack doesn't reply. It was difficult to gauge his emotions

even with the pumpkin, but at least he had his flames. Right now, I'm getting nothing.

"They were going to drag me away, but you saved me." I step over William's fallen corpse and place a hand over Jack's chest, my palm meeting hard muscle. "Thank you."

His satisfied rumble fills my heart with warmth, melting away a layer of tension. At least he understands I'm nothing like the hedge witch who tethered his soul to his body for the chaplain.

"How are you still here? I thought you had to leave at dawn."

"When I reached the gates of hell, they were closed." He removes his cloak and drapes it over my shoulders.

Warmth seeps into my skin. "Has that ever happened before?"

He makes a one-handed shrug. "Every year hell drags me back, but this is the first time in centuries I didn't kill an innocent."

My gaze wanders to William and the fallen police officers. If hell rejected him for sparing my life, surely he'll have to return tomorrow for murdering three men.

"What about them?"

"I do not share," he growls. "I will cut down the bastard who dares to touch what is mine."

"But you just killed them. Won't that get you in trouble?"

"My pistols only knocked out their souls."

"They're alive?"

"Aye." He points at the fallen officers. "The two in uniform procured young women for a brothel and performed acts against nature that have earned them a place in the second circle of hell."

My gaze wanders to William. "What about him?"

"I reaped his soul for forcing former sweethearts to fuck

other men."

My stomach plummets to the stone floor. Not at the thought that Jack is capable of extracting souls. That's probably part of his curse.

Was this what William was planning for me all along—to sleep with other men? Of course, it was. Marriage was the carrot he tried to use so I could service his uncles. After agreeing to something like that, things would have only gotten worse. At least now, I understand why those policemen didn't give a shit about my plight.

But there's one thing I don't understand.

"How do you know what they did?" I ask.

"All denizens of hell can see the crimes of their fellow sinners," he replies, sounding grave. "It is why I felt such deep sorrow each time the curse forced me to murder an innocent."

I give William's fallen body another kick. "Where's his soul?"

Jack holds up a squirming sack.

My nose wrinkles. "Why don't you release it to hell?"

"Because I want to perform a ritual of my own, but only with your permission."

"What do you mean?"

He cups the side of my face and draws the pad of his thumb over my cheekbone. The gesture is so tender that my chest aches with longing.

"Would you kiss me if I wore the face of a man you despise?" he asks.

I dart my gaze to William's fallen body, my pulse quickening. Earlier, while we were riding back to the stable yard, Jack mentioned wanting to do a lot more than give me a kiss. If I can fuck a ghost with the head of a pumpkin, I sure as hell could fuck him in William's body.

"You're going to possess my ex?"

"With your consent."

I gulp. "How will it work?"

"My ax extracted his filthy soul. His body is still very much alive."

"Possess him," I blurt. "But won't William become a ghost?"

"Leave him to me."

Jack carries William's body to the stone altar and draws symbols over his exposed skin with the officers' blood. I clasp the cloak around my neck, guessing that Jack learned this ritual from the man who cursed his soul. He probably picked up a lot of knowledge from centuries of reading the sins of other residents in hell.

He walks to the chest containing the gold sovereigns, chanting, "Nemo malus felix."

But when he empties the sack containing William's soul into the coins, my jaw drops.

William's going to haunt the gold.

Jack returns to William's body and pulls off his glove, revealing a transparent hand. He turns his whole body toward me as though asking a final question.

"Do it," I say.

He plunges his hand into William's chest, making his jacket deflate. After several heartbeats, his garments fall to the floor before vanishing. Even the cloak around my shoulders disappears into the ether.

William's body inhales a deep breath.

"Jack?"

I stumble forward just as he rises to sit. My heart beats so hard and fast I think I might expire. He has a body. He's alive.

"Bess." He stands, meeting me halfway.

The man looking down at me has William's arched brows, regal nose, and strong jaw, but there's nothing left of my ex-fiancé. His eyes are softer and his mouth is no longer sharp and cruel.

I place my hands on his chest, rise on my tiptoes, and search his blue eyes for flecks of fire. The intensity of his gaze is so penetrating that it touches my soul. This has to be him.

"Is that really you?" I ask, already knowing the answer.

"Aye," he replies, his deep voice echoing on the stone walls. He sounds nothing like William.

My heart flutters. "Jack, thank goodness."

"Let me look at you through living eyes," Jack says, his voice breathy, his gaze roaming my face. "I have waited two centuries for a taste of happiness, and I will wait no longer. Bess, may I kiss your sweet lips?"

"I told you before. You never need to ask."

Jack wraps an arm around my back and pulls me into his broad body. His heartbeat resounds across my chest, beating as fast as mine.

My breath quickens. My throat dries. My fingers tremble. The things we've done tonight are worthy of one of my steamy books, yet my heart flutters in anticipation of his lips.

He leans down, bringing our faces so close, seeming to savor the moment.

I'm so hungry for his touch that I rock forward and complete the kiss.

The first touch of his lips is like tiny forks of lightning that spread across my skin and race toward my heart. I fall against his broad chest and gasp. His tongue slips between my lips and curls against mine with delicious caresses.

Kissing Jack is nothing like kissing William. While my fiancé was lukewarm unless we reenacted a scene from one of my books, Jack is insistent, demanding, and possessive. It's as though he's committing me to memory.

The kiss grows deeper, harder, more urgent, and his

hand slides up my back to thread his fingers through my hair, holding me in place. His grip is deliciously tight with just enough tension to make my pussy pound.

I melt against his body and moan. I could kiss this man forever and it wouldn't be enough.

As the kiss continues, my head spins, and it feels like I'm riding through a sky of diamonds. Darkness creeps along the edges of my vision, making me sway on my feet—I need to breathe.

He pulls back, and I blink away the stars.

"Bloody hell, that was hot," I whisper, my voice hoarse.

"It was heaven," he murmurs, his smile making the corners of his eyes crinkle. "You taste so sweet, my beautiful Bess."

We stand chest to chest, sharing the same air, our hearts beating in unison. Jack's erection presses into my belly, filling my pussy with heat.

"Fuck." I slip my hand down to his breeches. "I need you so much."

Jack grabs my wrist. "No."

I flinch. "What?"

He gazes down at me, his expression earnest. "You deserve better than a hard fuck in the place where my soul was once tethered. I only brought you here because it was where my magic was strongest."

"Oh."

"I'm no longer confined to this area."

"Could you take over William's life?"

Jack grimaces. "There is much I need to learn about this century."

"I'll teach you!"

He threads his fingers through mine and smiles.

"Come on," I say with a burst of joy that touches my soul. "I'll drive you back to the manor."

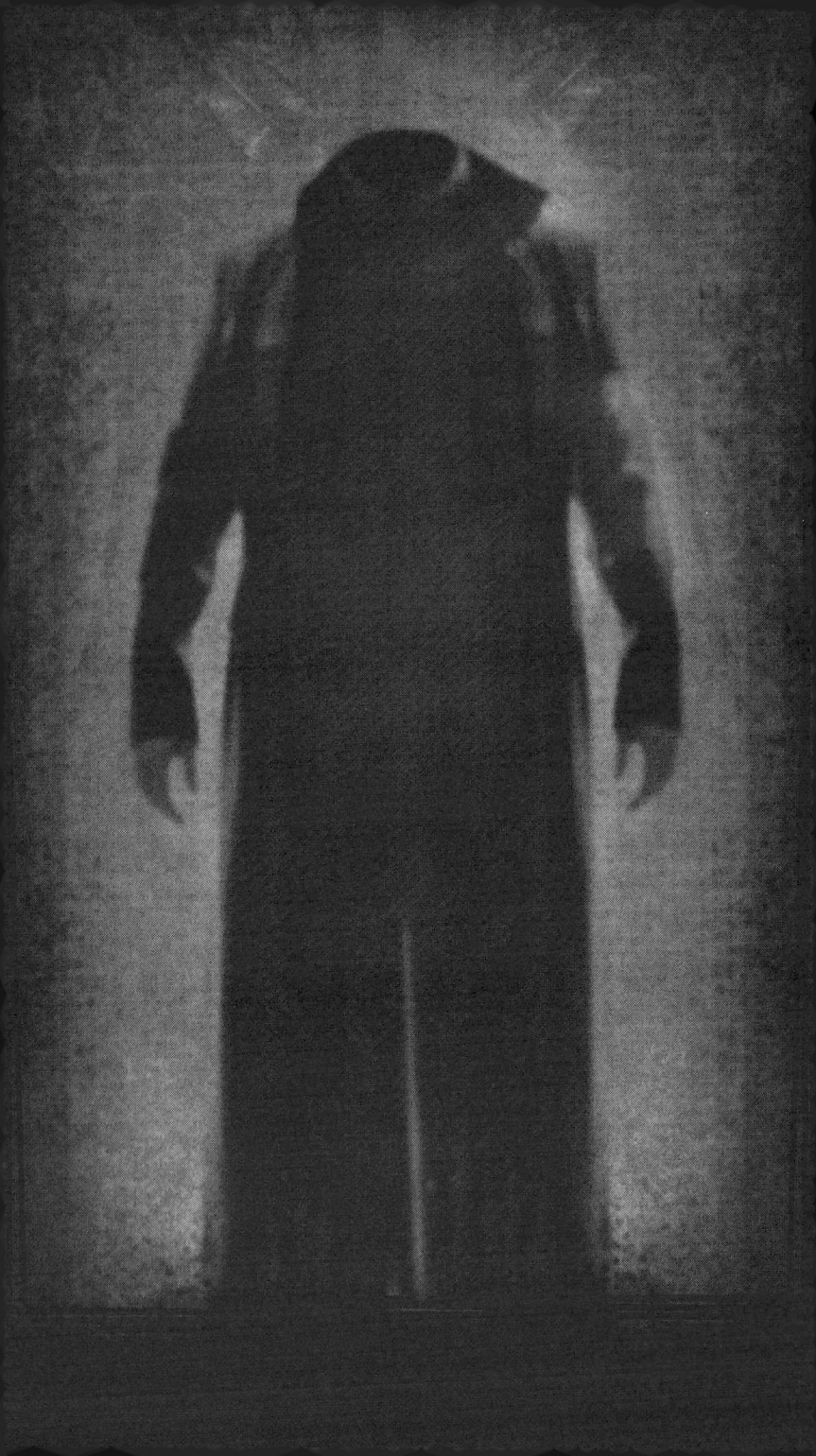

Chapter Thirteen

~~~

T he sun is rising as I drive William's Mercedes to the grounds of Whitechapel Manor. By now, all the guests' cars are gone, save for a black Bentley. My jaw tightens. It looks like we might encounter one of William's uncles.

Jack and I decided to leave the soulless officers and their vehicle at the cemetery. Ghostly bullets leave no entry or exit wounds, and whoever stumbles on them can make their own assumptions.

I park outside the double doors and steal a glance at Jack for his reaction to the huge brick building. He doesn't notice that he's become a wealthy man—he's too busy staring at the side of my face.

"Are you alright?" I ask.

"Your hair looks like flames in the daylight," he murmurs.

I reach for my braid. "Is that good or bad?"

"It's ravishing." He takes my hand and brings my knuckles to his lips. "Just like you."

My eyelids flutter shut. I want to bask in his affection and bathe in his admiration. William's love language was gift-giving but felt more like bribery. I've only known Jack for a few hours, but he's already a perfect package of words of affirmation, physical touch, and acts of service.

I place my hand on his. "One of William's uncles is still inside."

"I sense both of them."

"How?" I shake my head, already knowing the answer. "Because of the time you spent in hell."

He nods.

"Stay quiet until you've perfected William's posh accent. We don't want his uncle thinking anything's wrong."

The corner of Jack's mouth lifts into a half smirk.

Just as I'm about to add something else, the front door swings open. Thomas steps out, wearing William's burgundy dressing gown. The fabric distorts around his huge body, riding up so anyone can see his balls.

I clench my teeth. "Fuck."

"You never need to worry about him." Jack gives my hand a gentle squeeze.

Thomas jogs to the car, his cheeks flushed. "What took you so long, boy?" He peers through the tinted window and barks a laugh. "I thought you would return her to us hand-cuffed. How did you convince her to drive you back?"

My jaw clenches at the confirmation of William's intentions, and I pull my borrowed cloak shut. I hope my fiancé enjoys an eternity of being split into hundreds of gold coins.

I open the car door, making sure to hit Thomas in the gut. He stumbles back with a grunt.

"William changed his mind," I snap. "He doesn't want to share."

Thomas peers at Jack, his brow furrowed. "You can say goodbye to that one-percent share."

I clench my fists, remembering how the uncles meddle in everything related to Whitechapel Finance. "This was the plan all along? To sell me so William could control fifty-one percent of the firm?"

Thomas doesn't even spare me a glance. Because to men like him, I'm just a commodity. Jack sweeps his arm toward the manor, and the two of them walk through the front door.

I trust Jack not to agree with Thomas, but I don't trust him not to shoot him with one of his pistols where we might get caught by Samuel. It's too late to say anything, so I follow them inside.

Samuel strolls down the grand staircase, still dressed in his highwayman's cloak. He places a hand over his mouth and yawns. "About time. We'll have her here."

Nodding, Jack gestures at them to stand at the foot of the stairs.

"Forming a line?" Thomas asks with a laugh and joins his brother.

Jack grins.

I glance down at the pistols on Jack's gun belt and gulp. His uncles are so preoccupied with the prospect of their blowjobs that they don't even notice the weapons aren't part of a costume. Can he shoot them both without one of them attacking? Jack's new body is more slender than his ghostly form. Thomas could flatten us both in a stampede.

Before I can whisper a warning, Jack materializes his double-headed ax and swings at their necks

"Fuck," I yell.

The two men tumble to their knees before falling flat on their faces. By the time I turn to Jack, the ax is already gone.

"Are they in hell?" I ask.

"Not yet." Jack holds up two squirming sacks.

I step back, my nose wrinkling. This is just like what he

did with William, except there's no horny ghost to step into their bodies. I bite down on the inside of my cheek. "Can their bodies survive like that?"

"Long enough so it won't be murder."

Jack tosses the sacks over his shoulder, and they disappear with two puffs of sulfur-scented smoke. Before I can ask about their sins, he scoops me into his arms and cradles me to his chest.

I cling onto his neck and shriek, "What are you doing?"

Jack's ghostly body was about seven feet tall with the pumpkin, and he made me feel like a doll. The form he inhabits is six-four, muscular, but not overly bulky. I guess I'm not used to being carried.

"I'm jealous," he growls.

"Why?"

"My ax got to taste your cunt, as did my pistols. It's my turn."

Tingles spread across my skin and settle between my thighs. I squeeze them together and groan, "Upstairs."

Jack crosses the hallway, hopping over the fallen bodies, and takes the steps two at a time.

I glance over his shoulder at Thomas's hairy ass and grimace. "Are you sure they'll still be breathing by the time we've finished?"

"Worry more about how I plan on filling all your holes with cum!"

Laughing, I guide Jack through the hallway and to the master suite. It feels strange to bring him to William's bedroom, even though he inhabits his body, but I toss the discomfort aside. After this round of sex, we need to go downstairs and deal with the soulless perverts.

Jack carries me through the bedroom and lowers me on the mahogany four poster. I land on the mattress with a gentle thud. He pulls off his gloves and climbs to my side.

Daylight streams through the window, illuminating the side of his face. His eyes are darker and at the core of each blue iris is a starburst of gold. For a moment, I see a different man—one who is kinder, more compassionate, and one who wants me without condition.

"I will spend the rest of my existence thanking you for my freedom." His voice trembles and he runs a hand up my exposed thigh. "I have been plucked from the inferno to dine at the gates of heaven."

"You're hungry?" I ask, my breath quickening.

"Only for you." He slides his hands on my knees. "Now, open up those gates."

Relaxing my legs I let Jack slide his hands down my inner thighs. The touch of his bare hands makes me shiver with desire. I need his mouth. I need his tongue. I need Jack.

"I wanted to do this to you the moment we met," he says, his eyes burning.

"Even with the curse?" I whisper.

"No amount of magic could blind me to your charms. When your tits spilled out, sensation rushed to my cock, and when you stroked it." He groans. "Bess, your touch is a miracle."

"I'm so glad you're free, but how long will it last?"

He shakes his head. "Let us enjoy this moment."

"Alright."

He's right. If Jack's soul stays attached to William's body, it will buy us plenty of time to research. The man who cursed him is responsible for the deaths of all the innocents. He's the one who deserves a place in hell, not Jack. All those thoughts come to an abrupt stop when his warm breath fans over my pussy.

"Wet for me, my little beauty?"

"Always," I murmur.

He spreads my legs wider, putting me on full display.

My cheeks heat. Now that I'm no longer fucking for survival, a part of me is scandalized that I'm showing my pussy to a man I've barely known for a night.

Those thoughts dissolve the moment he swipes his tongue up my slit.

"You taste as sweet as you look," he groans.

My legs spasm, but Jack holds them further apart. The next lick jolts me with a current of arousal that makes my back arch.

"Fuck," I say from between clenched teeth.

Jack licks a path up and down my pussy, savoring me like I'm his favorite dessert. He traces a tight circle at my opening then slides his tongue to loop around my swollen clit.

On and on, he goes at a steady, unhurried pace that makes my toes curl. There's just enough pressure to send sparks across my skin but not enough to make me cum.

"Jack," I say, my voice breaking. "Please."

"Tell me what you want, sweet Bess."

"Y-your tongue on my clit." I pause, wondering if that word was invented in the 18th century, and add, "My nub."

"Ahh." He rises from between my legs and grins.

"Why did you stop?" I ask.

"Sounds like you should ride my face."

My eyes widen. "Really?"

Jack takes hold of my hips and flips me over, so I'm on my hands and knees, showing him my ass and pussy. Jack places a kiss on my inner thigh and settles on the mattress between my legs.

"Smother me like a good girl," he rumbles. "Use me as your saddle."

Shuffling around on the mattress, I arrange myself so I'm facing the huge tent in his breeches. My chest reverberates with a groan of gratitude. Somehow, this new body of his has a generous length and girth. I lower myself onto his face, placing my weight on my thighs. He only just got a living body, and the last thing I want for him is to suffocate.

"Bess," he growls, his hot breath warming my folds. "I told you to sit."

Relaxing my leg muscles, I cover his face with my ass and pussy, muffling Jack's pleasured groans. This time, when he licks up and down my slit, I move against his tongue, letting my clit chase the sensations.

Jack gets the hint and flicks the tip of his tongue back and forth over my clit, making me shiver. I bear down on him, increasing the pressure, and bite back a groan. This is so fucking hot. William always wanted control during oral sex. Now, I get to cum all over that face.

As Jack's lips clamp around my clit, my stomach dips, and he sucks hard enough to reap my soul.

"J-Jack," I yell.

I can't hear whatever he says around my pussy, because I'm panting too loud, whimpering, wriggling, writhing on his face as he drives me close to the edge.

Jack's hips hump the air, his erection straining through his pants. It's looking longer and thicker than anything I'd seen before on my ex. I fumble at his button, pull down his zipper, and reach into his silk boxers.

He groans around my clit, sending vibrations across my pussy and down my thighs.

Fuck.

I'm so close.

Clenching my teeth, I ease his erection out from a pair of silk boxers. I cry out to find it's nearly the same as Jack's original cock. Precum streams from the tip and drenches my fingers. I stroke up and down, matching the movements of his tongue.

His groan makes the muscles of my pussy clench. I hope

his refractory period is as impressive as the size of his cock because I want to ride him after watching him spurt.

Pressure builds up around my clit, and my toes curl tighter than fists. Jack increases the suction while lashing my clit with the tip of his tongue. Fuck. I want this to last all morning, but there's only so much a woman can resist.

My clit throbs from all the attention, and the muscles of my pussy tighten, desperate to be filled. Jack makes a low, appreciative groan that pushes me over the edge.

Sensation rushes through my system like a tidal wave, threatening to drown me in liquid ecstasy. I clench and shudder, my fingers tightening around his cock. Spots dance before my eyes, and my mind goes blank. I have to squeeze my eyes shut to ride through the overwhelming pleasure.

"Fuck, Bess, you cum so prettily," I'm sure Jack says.

My hands quicken around his shaft until he climaxes with a muffled roar.

I open my eyes, finding him spurting a jet of creamy cum. Lurching forward, I close my lips around his thick cockhead, and let the warm fluid hit the back of my throat. I swallow over and over, but there's so much that it spills down the sides of my mouth.

Even the way he climaxes is more erotic than William.

As the waves of my orgasm recede, I try to rise from Jack's face, but he grabs my hips and pushes me back into place.

"Where do you think you're going?" he growls. "I haven't finished."

Jack laps up my release, making me twitch with my orgasm's aftershocks. I make myself comfortable on his face and sigh. This is better than any fairytale. Thanks to Jack, I have control of the firm. I also have financial security and a future. Most importantly, I have a man who appreciates everything about me. A man who would never share me with another.

This really is the best Halloween surprise.

Epilogue

Seven Years Later

The silk mask slips down my left eye. Frowning in the bedroom mirror, I tighten it around the back. This Halloween, I'm dressed as a faerie, complete with pointed ears.

"That's better." I step back and admire my ball gown.

It's emerald green with a lace neckline that curls around my shoulders like the tendrils of a pumpkin stalk. Its skirt is full but lightweight because I already know this Halloween party will be chaotic.

The bathroom door opens, and Jack steps out, dressed in a forest green frock coat embroidered in gold lace. He wears his hair longer, with gentle waves that soften his features.

Jack's features now resemble the handsome face I saw in the flames, and there's now barely a trace of William. The change was so gradual that barely anyone noticed.

It's not like Jack runs in the same social circles as William. Everyone thinks he had some kind of breakdown when his uncles 'fell ill.'

My gaze drifts down to the tan riding breeches that hug his muscular thighs. All that horse riding has given him an incredible physique.

He crosses the room and scowls. "The veil between life and death wears thin."

I smooth down the silk cravat he wears beneath the jacket. "And you're a living, breathing man who will enjoy a long and happy life."

A muscle in his jaw flexes. Jack gets anxious every Halloween, even though he's no longer a ghost compelled by a malevolent curse. It doesn't matter how much I assure him that he's safe, a part of him still believes the magic will drag him back to hell.

I wrap my arms around his neck and pull him into a hug. "This year won't be any different from the last seven."

"Aye," he mutters.

Drawing back, I gaze into his deep blue eyes. His irises are even darker, with golden flecks that still resemble flames. They're a constant reminder of his unjust punishment.

"Have you done anything this year to deserve a place in hell?" I ask.

He shakes his head.

"Are you planning anything reckless?"

The corners of his lips twitch. "No."

"Then don't worry." I offer him a smile. "If this gorgeous body is soulless tomorrow at dawn, I'll crack open a ouija board and stuff you back inside."

His grin makes my heart turn a somersault. "What did I ever do to deserve you?"

"Spared my life." I rock forward on my tiptoes and give him a peck on the lips. "Gave me mind-blowing sex." I reach down between our bodies and cup his hardening cock. "Protected me from predators. Fathered the most beautiful little boy and girl."

"Bess." He leans down and captures my mouth in a kiss.

Jack's lips are urgent, insistent, demanding, as though this might be our last day together. After centuries of suffering, I can't blame him for not believing his change in fortune.

Pulling his cock out of his breeches, I kiss back with equal heat, trying to communicate with my body what I can't with words. No matter what, Jack will never return to hell.

After taking over William's body, Jack and I spent the night celebrating. In the morning, we called an ambulance to carry away his soulless but breathing uncles. Their bodies are still on life support and no longer able to meddle in the affairs of Whitechapel Finance.

Jack and I had a Christmas wedding in the manor, making me the firm's joint owner. Work hasn't changed all that much because I still manage the business with him as its figurehead.

"I need you," he groans.

Arousal fills my pussy with molten heat. I wrap my arms around his shoulders and moan. "We still have time."

With so much money at our disposal, it was easy to research the curse. We discovered that the chaplain who condemned Jack to purge the highways of robbers was part of a fraternity that dabbled in the occult. All its members were long dead, but we tracked down some of their artifacts, including a sacred text. We purchased everything related to the fraternity, consulted academics, and even hired mediums.

According to the lore, Jack will be tethered to William's body and then grow old like any other person. And when he dies, he'll go to heaven or hell based on his actions during this lifetime.

It's a wonderful second chance—not just for him.

The best part is that the four other souls he extracted from their bodies belonged to hell-bound sinners. William's uncles ran a Ponzi scheme that preyed on the vulnerable, and the things they did to young women wanted me to cut off their dicks. Jack and I arranged for a coin dealer to sell the gold sovereigns to private collectors, and we donated the proceeds to a charity that provides safe houses for women in desperate need.

His kisses travel down my neck, each touch of his lips detonating tiny explosions of bliss. He gathers up my skirt around my waist, hooks his arm beneath my thighs, and lifts me off my feet.

"Jack," I say with a giggle.

He silences me with his lips and carries me over to the wall. "I'm going to fuck you hard and fast," he mumbles around the kiss. "Then I'm going to pump you full of my cum. If you spill so much as a drop, I'll fill you with more."

"Then I'll make sure to let it trickle down my leg."

He pins me against the hard surface and growls, "No knickers? My wife is a wanton little wench."

"Easy access." I bite his lip and buck my hips, and rub my swollen clit back and forth against the ridge of his cock-head. "Now, stop talking like a man from the eighteenth century and give me that big dick."

Jack's nostrils flares, as do the gold flecks in his irises. Before I can consider if it's a trick of the light, he shoves into me with a hard thrust.

Pleasure explodes across my pussy, accompanied by a delicious stretch. I tighten my legs around his hips and groan. When he pulls back I dig my fingers into his shoulders and hold my breath.

Jack thrusts back into me, deep and hard. I throw my head back and pant. He pounds into me with firm and fast strokes, just as promised. Sex with Jack is always terrific, whether it's in the bed, against a wall, or bent over a breeding bench. The only thing that would make this hotter would be a plug up the ass, but we're already running late for the party.

With each thrust, Jack hits my clit, electrifying my nerves with sparks of rapture. My pussy clenches and spasms around his girth, making me see stars. I want to tell him how good he feels, but I can barely breathe, let alone form words.

"You're taking my cock so well," he snarls into my ear. "Such a good girl."

I make a noise in the back of my throat.

Even after seven years, those words still hit the spot.

"You're so wet, so tight, so mine."

"Yours," I try to say.

"If I let you cum, you're going to be quiet, understand?"

I squeeze my eyes shut and groan. That's going to be impossible when he's pounding into me with all his strength. Lizzie and John might be busy downstairs at the party, but I don't trust them not to come searching for us upstairs.

"Bess," he says, his voice sharp. "Promise to make no noise, or I won't let you cum."

"O-okay," I moan.

"You remember your training?"

I give him an eager nod. How could I ever forget? Jack's pony antics usually involve some kind of edging before I'm allowed to cum at his command. Thank fuck he's in a hurry.

"Five," he says, starting the countdown.

My pulse quickens. I grind my hips, trying to increase the friction.

"Four... Three.... Two..."

A knock sounds on the door.

"Mr. and Mrs. Whitechapel?" asks the party planner.

"The catering staff has cleared the kid's buffet and set up the games. Will you be joining us for apple bobbing?"

"C-coming," I say through clenched teeth as the orgasm gallops through me like a herd of wild horses.

"Alright, Ma'am, I'll tell them to wait," she replies.

Jack continues fucking, adding a stampede of sensation that makes my eyes roll toward the back of my head. I take another deep breath, but he clamps a hand over my mouth.

"Quiet," he hissed.

As her footsteps disappear down the hallway, Jack's strokes become erratic. His entire body tightens, and he comes with a quiet shudder. I cling to Jack, breathing hard through the rest of my climax.

"Thank you," he pulls out and sets me back on my feet. I lean against the wall, my legs still trembling. "This time of year brings everything back."

I cup the side of his face. "If you want, I'll call back the planner and we can—"

"No." He kisses my forehead. "Being inside you chases away that sense of doom. Let's go downstairs."

"Promise me you'll say something if it comes back."

"Promise." Jack wraps an arm around my waist. "Are we riding tomorrow?"

My pussy tightens at the promise of getting bent over the breeding bench.

"That depends on if I'll get sugar lumps."

He places another kiss on my lips. "Only the best for my beautiful Bess."

Jack installed a heated tack room on the grounds for pony play. His magic faded a few days after settling into William's body, so he can no longer create illusions, pistols, or ghostly axes. He can't even see people's sins.

We step out of the master suite and into the hallway to the strains of *The Monster Mash*. Neither of us likes lavish parties, but everything changes when you have children.

"Mum, Dad!" yells a little voice as we reach the bottom of the stairs.

A six-year-old Wicked Witch of the West sprints down the hallway, her robes flying. The green face paint has already worn off around her mouth, presumably from the buffet.

Jack steps forward, gathers her in his arms, swings her around, and laughs. "Got you, my pretty!"

It's the same laugh he made after slicing off the top of my car, reminding me of the Halloween night when my life finally began.

The clank of metal hitting the marble floor turns my attention back to the hallway, where a miniature Tin Man picks up a stainless steel funnel and pops it back on his head. Then he ambles toward us like a broken robot.

"John," I say with a laugh.

My five-year-old son tilts up his silver-painted face. "Where have you been? You're late for the games."

"Sorry. Daddy and I are here now." I take John's hand and give it a gentle squeeze.

We're usually present for our children, but Halloween always reminds Jack of nights he'd rather forget. Then there's the whole trauma of having spent so much time in Hell... The first few years, he would wake up in the middle of the night with cold sweats. Spending time with horses is therapeutic, but there's only so much a person can do after centuries of punishment.

If anyone deserves redemption, it's Jack.

He sets Lizzie on her feet, and the four of us make our way to the party. I cast my gaze over them, my heart bursting.

Seven years ago, when I walked out of Whitechapel

Manor, I thought my life was over. If anyone ever told me happiness would come in the form of an ax-murdering ghost, I'd ask what they'd been smoking.

I send the pieces of William a silent word of gratitude. Thanks to him, I have the perfect lover and family.

END

Also by Siggy Shade

Paranormal Romance:

Tentacle Entanglement

Stalked by the Boogie Man

Swallowing Water

❀

Contemporary Romance

Wicked Lessons

Printed in Great Britain
by Amazon